I0654344

BLUE

DANCER

AND

THE

DARK

BY

LINDA MCKOWN

Publisher LindaMcKownAuthor LLC

Scottsdale, AZ

1

Blue Dancer and the Dark

ISBN-13: 978-1-7344095-6-7

Library of Congress Control Number: 2021913748

Author:
LindaMcKownAuthor LLC
11574 E Running Deer Trail
Scottsdale, AZ 85262
https://www.lindamckown.com

Any names of people and entities are fictitious in this story having been created by the author's imagination.

The Front Cover Photo of the book was purchased from Shutterstock. Joseph McKown did book cover choice and editing.

Dreams matter because sometimes that is all we have in this life. Most have more dreams than others. This book is for those people who have dreams in their hearts and the willingness to believe. They are the incredibly special ones.

To my husband who allowed me to dream and came along for the wonderful ride.

Table of Contents

1 The Dance Poster

Gloria Strand stopped on the street next to a gray brick building. She saw the large colorful poster under the glass with gold and black letters. She touched the glass.

"My dream can come true."

The poster was advertising the Columbia Dancing Troupe's tryouts in New York City. The female dancer in the poster wore a beautiful crown in her updo hair. The male dancer stood proudly beside her. The costumes were gorgeous royal blue velvet, gold braid, white tulle, and tan spandex. Their bodies were toned muscle.

As she was reading the bulletin, she saw the royal blue logo. Gloria rubbed her fingers on the glass to trace the design. She closed her eyes for a moment and smiled.

A woman walked out of the Columbia building and noticed the young woman with her eyes closed while touching the poster. She was a dancer and stopped. Her royal blue jacket contained the logo as an emblem. The woman talked with Gloria about the dance company. She asked why the young woman stopped.

"The poster is beautiful."

The dancer looked at the poster and back at the young woman.

"My name is Bella Reine. I'm the first string. Do you dance?"

"I'm Gloria Strand, and I love to dance. I would rather dance than eat."

Bella liked the dancer's enthusiasm which was half the battle. She encouraged her to apply.

"Don't ever let anyone stop you from your dream. Be brave and go for the gold crown. If there's no crown, pick the diamond tiara."

"Thank you. I will enter the tryouts."

Gloria wrote down the website information, left the building filled with inspiration, and went to a coffee shop.

Sipping a latte, she believed the poster was a gift. If she had chosen a different street, she would have missed the tryout information. Once home, she immediately went online and submitted her resume. This was the last day to apply. Gloria's fingers shook as she quickly hit the send button.

She wanted the crown. More than anything, she wanted to dance with this company. Looking in the window reflection at home, the young woman quietly repeated over and over.

"I will be a Columbia dancer. Please, please, please!"

With her new blue dance outfit on order, she waited. The cost of the outfit was a month's wages. She wanted to be prepared in case the troupe required dance videos.

"A little sparkle never hurt. Diamonds will someday work in a crown."

Three days passed. Gloria dressed and breathed in the morning air. The weather was clear today and a good sign of a pretty day unfolding.

"The blue sky is more cobalt than my outfit."

Getting a job with this prestigious company could help further her career in the traditional ballet world.

"I need to get to practice. Stop wasting time and skip breakfast."

Gloria drove to the dance studio and began her stretches. She was at practice when her friend, Geri Sullivan, called. Her towel was placed over her neck as she answered her cell phone.

"Where are you, Geri? I thought we were supposed to practice together today."

"Guess what I received in the mail? The envelope was white and long. There were gold and black letters."

Gloria walked toward the locker area. She was half-listening to her friend's chatter. Locker number ten was in front of her.

"Silly, most envelopes are white and long. People use black ink more frequently than blue. Not sure about the gold. I'll guess what was in the envelope. There were coupons for free hamburgers at Joey's Place. Extra onions included. Their sign is gold."

Her friend wrinkled her nose. Gloria could imagine her friend's offended face.

"Ha, ha. Sometimes the envelopes are tan. I hate Joey's hamburgers, and you know it. They use too much onion even when I ask for *no onions*. Half their onions are burned. How can a person burn onions on a flat grill? Flat grills smoke when something is burning. Plus, they have dorks for employees."

"Yes, their employees like to bug you. Either your New Yorker accent is to blame, or it's the weird kid from our high school? He did have a crush on you."

"How come you don't have an accent?"

Gloria laughed.

"My mother wanted me to sound normal."

Geri ignored the dig. Gloria remembered the envelope.

"Okay, I give, what was in the mail?"

Geri shrieked, "I'm so excited."

Gloria pulled the phone away from her ear.

"Geri, stop screaming?"

"The letter is from the Columbia Dancing Troupe."

Gloria stopped putting her stuff in the bag.

"The troupe sent me an invitation to submit my dancing videos and portrait. The deadline for submittal of the two items is three weeks."

Gloria knew once the videos were received, the dance judges would select the dancers for their next season's tour. The tour would start in six weeks.

She screamed into the phone.

"Get Out!"

"Yes, can you believe they want to see me dance? The thrill of receiving the invitation and making it this far is awesome. Oh, I'm using Rory Randall as my video photographer. I know he is expensive, but the man walks on water and is a wizard in the business. He will also take a large photograph with me surrounded by red roses and yellow lilies next week. My dad wants a picture to put in his office. Of course, the florist must order the lilies as overnight delivery."

Gloria hated to ask for Mr. Randall's prices.

"I just submitted my application three days ago. My application was sent on the last day."

Gloria bit her lip and looked puzzled. Her friend never told her about the open tryouts. Yet, she failed to tell her friend about her application. Geri babbled on, and Gloria became apprehensive.

"If you get an acceptance letter from the troupe, promise me you will pay the five thousand dollars for any required videos and photographs. Besides the photographer is older and cute. He will give us a recommendation letter, too. I belong in this troupe. Correction, we belong in this troupe. They will be our ticket to the big time."

Gloria was surprised at the cost. She forgave her friend and herself for not telling each other about the tryouts. The young dancer leaned against the locker rubbing her forehead.

"Whew, this Rory person is expensive. Is there anyone else cheaper?"

Her friend sighed. Geri knew money wasn't always plentiful in the Strand household.

"I can loan you some money. My dad won't mind. He knows you are good and will pay him back."

Gloria opened the cheap lock. There was a sound of metal on metal.

"No, I have some money."

Geri was glad.

"You need to check the photographer out. Like I said, if you want to make the top, you must pick the best. His reputation will sell the judges on your videos and of course, your lithe and beautiful body will complete the package. Speaking of bodies, my outfit arrived today. I look hot."

Gloria couldn't help but giggle.

"You are so full of it."

The two women worked at the same gym and did their routines at the same dance studio which was usually six days out of a week.

They knew each other's strengths and weaknesses. As best friends, they helped each other and shared dance knowledge most of the time. She pushed her hair out of her eyes as she undid her ponytail. The black one was dropped in the bag, and a pink tie was placed on her wrist. Doubt filled her mind.

"What if I don't get an invitation? Oh, man, I'll be super crushed."

"Gloria, you mustn't worry. We went to an elite and top-notch dance school. We've got the credentials and years of experience with classes. The instructors are well known in New York. There's nothing to fear. The judges just need to see you dance. You look thin but can pack a wallop. This is now both our dreams."

She took her bag out and shut the locker door with a bang.

"Thanks for reminding me. You have the rich girl's address and impressive daddy lawyer. He works with international clients. My father wears an apron and throws patrons out the front door when the time reaches one in the morning. Amazingly, they always come back because he has a free hotdog with all the fixings and popcorn every Friday night at the bistro."

"I do love your dad's hotdog spread. He makes the best pickle relish."

She found her car keys and groaned.

"He mixes cans of stuff, puts the junk in a blender, and calls the relish homemade. The secret is sweet pickles, mustard, garlic, a touch of sugar, jarred peppers, and celery seed."

Geri could hear a car start. She looked in the wall mirror at her costume as she held the cloth to her body. She swung back and forth.

"Those flavors work for me. Your dad puts the thin red onions in a separate dish. He's an angel and not a dork. Plus, he doesn't burn stuff, and he's always available to talk."

Gloria glanced at her watch.

"Look, I've got to run. I'm on duty at my dad's place in fifteen minutes. He told me I was late yesterday and the day before. But he doesn't mind. I'll explain the dance troupe might want two videos and photographs. Oh, my meeting with a dancer named Bella from the troupe and seeing the poster at the same time was a pure coincidence. She was a doll and sweet when I talked with her. I'll tell you later what she said."

Gloria put her cell phone in the car's center console and drove to the restaurant. There would someday be an invitation, or there wouldn't be an invitation in her mailbox.

She looked at the small sign out front, *Gloria's Bistro*. Her father changed the name from Estelle to his daughter's name when her parents got their divorce. She drove to the parking lot in the back. The dust enveloped her car. She waited a few seconds before opening the door.

When her mother died, the money was given to Gloria for her dancing lessons and schooling. She looked at her bank account yesterday. The amount left was eight thousand dollars.

"I need to get accepted with this troupe or quit dancing."

Entry-level dancers started at two hundred thousand dollars for a twenty-city tour that lasted a year.

Leaving her vehicle, she went into the back kitchen. She washed her hands. Grabbing her apron and placing the white cloth over her black tights and black knit top, she kicked off her soft contemporary dance shoes.

She added her thick white socks and rolled them down. The hot pink tennis shoes were slipped on, and the straps moved in place.

Putting her long dishwater blonde hair back into a ponytail using a pink headband, she was ready to tackle the crowd. She was assigned to the beer tap, pop, and coffee section tonight.

The wood half-doors were pushed open. She was greeted with blue and white balloons tied with gold ribbon, happy faces, and raised glasses in the bistro main room.

"Surprise!"

Her father came rushing over and handed her an envelope. The seal ripped on one end, and there were tire tracks on the outside of the envelope.

"We pulled the letter out of the end because we saw the post people ruined the envelope. We were worried about the letter getting damaged. The letter survived. Honey, I did read your letter."

Gloria saw the envelope was white and long with black and gold letters. She looked at her father's beaming face.

"Sweetheart, you've been invited to submit your dancing videos to the Columbia Dancing Troupe."

The bistro patrons clapped their approval and cheered.

2 Invitation Party

Her father handed her the one-page letter. Gloria quickly scanned the document. She touched the royal blue logo. Her stunned smile grew wider.

"I received an invitation from the Columbia Dancing Troupe. Tell me that I'm not dreaming, or I shall faint dead away?"

Her father frowned.

"Don't faint; the letter is real," offered Guy.

Gloria looked at the balloons and people. Tears came to her eyes.

One of the patrons hollered, "Guy, we don't have all day. Put her on the countertop. We want to see some of her fancy dancing."

Her father looked at Gloria. She put the letter and envelope on the corkboard behind the counter. She nodded.

Two burly men picked Gloria up and deposited her on top of the polished wood.

The bistro waiter brought her recorder machine out from under the bar and selected the fast-paced song.

"Thanks, Stan."

Gloria began her routine that she practiced for this exact moment. Every day she tightened the steps to fit the length and width of her father's countertop. The patrons stepped back giving Gloria room for her legs to swing, kick, and do splits.

They clapped to the beat of the music. The door to the bistro filled with onlookers.

15

Gloria was in heaven watching her friends smiling and shaking hands with other people she knew who recently walked in. The patrons were bobbing with the beat. Guy threw his daughter a clean cloth towel. Gloria held the towel over her head like a queen holding a piece of expensive silk.

Gloria started singing the song and motioned for the patrons to join with her. Stan and Guy joined in. The patrons knew the song because she played the song whenever she worked. The song was number one on her recorder.

This song was what woke her up in the morning and started the fire within her heart and feet. She knew most everyone in the bistro. They were her audience since she was seven.

Their boisterous encouragement wiped away any fear of performing in front of people. She ended in a sit spin with her arms raised. Stan popped a balloon, and paper confetti poured over her. The confetti fell on the bar and floor. The song ended, and the burly men helped her return to solid ground. Stan turned the volume down on the recorder and let the rest of Gloria's songs play.

She knocked the confetti out of her hair and top. Her face was flushed and happy.

The neighborhood baker brought over a huge chocolate cake with white frosting and her name was splashed in blue with edible gold drizzled on the top like confetti. There was a cardboard gold crown on plastic pillars. The baker removed the crown and handed it to Gloria. She adjusted the crown on her head.

The chef cut the cake which was placed on paper plates along with plastic forks and blue napkins.

Cheese and sliced meat trays were brought out with veggie trays and dip to feed the hungry crowd of friends. The Italian restaurant down the block brought large baskets of fresh breadsticks and various dishes of meat and meatless sauces. Not to be outdone, the Chinese restaurant brought fried crab wontons in large bamboo containers and chips with sweet and sour dipping sauce.

Stan grabbed the real plates from under the counter to help the patrons handle the extra food items. The men shoved the tables together to leave the bar free for the drinks. Gloria didn't need to work because her father called in extra waiters for the celebration and cleanup.

At one o'clock in the morning, they ushered the patrons out the front door. The food was all gone except for a bag and a half of Chinese chips. The two servers and cook loaded the dishwasher and left. Gloria and her dad sat down to talk over coffee. The floor was strewn with paper confetti.

"What a heck of a fun time! I'm glad people came here to help us celebrate. The restaurants were a surprise with free food. The Chinese restauranteur left us two jars of his sweet and sour sauce for tomorrow's noon crowd with a bunch of business cards and more chips. The Italian place gave us a bowl of matches with their business name."

"Good advertising," mentioned Gloria.

"I gave them short notice about the letter, and they stopped what they were doing. No one wanted to miss giving you their congratulations and seeing your special dance. We've been bragging about this moment for three days."

He handed her a large mason jar with money.

"My patrons, a few strangers, and the businesses donated toward your videos. We counted two thousand dollars, and I put in a thousand."

"Thank you, dad. We need to put out a huge sign tomorrow expressing our thanks to them for their generosity."

Guy went and pulled a white cardboard sign from behind the freezer in the back room. He showed her the sign with the words, *Gloria loves and sends her thanks to everyone.* There was a stencil drawing of a blue ballet dancer in high flight. Her father caught one of her favorite moves.

Gloria clapped her hands. She hugged her dad for thinking of everything to speed her career along.

"Maybe we should add a neon dancer to our front sign. We could market the blue dancer thing."

"Slow down, dad. The judges must approve my dance routines."

"They will. You are the best dancer that I've ever seen. You have wings and grace as your mom did. They will choose you."

Gloria knew her mother danced in a nightclub a long time ago.

"Now, what are you going to do about the videos? They want a slow modern dance routine and a fast ballet dance routine at a minimum of four minutes. I only know our part-time server, Stan Martin. His girlfriend bought him a nice video camera last year. However, as a photographer, he shoots the ceiling a lot."

She sighed.

"Professional photographers are expensive."

"I'm thinking you need a better and more experienced person."

She didn't know. Her thoughts wandered.

"Geri received her letter three days ago."

Her father squeezed Gloria's hand.

"Well, there is no surprise in her getting the same letter. She's been here in my bistro since twelve and entertained my patrons. Geri is good, but not as good as my daughter. Your mind remembers the steps."

"Thanks again, Dad, but you are prejudiced. However, the compliments help boost my confidence. Geri mentioned a professional man named Rory Randall. I don't know him. He will cut two videos for me and print three eight by ten photos plus provide a letter of recommendation. The problem is his price is five thousand dollars. I do have the money, especially now with the mason jar fund."

"Then, you must contact this person first thing in the morning. If Geri is using him, he must have a good reputation. Her father is fussy. This is your mother's dream as well as mine and your own. She would want you to spend the money. I want you to look impressive. Knock them dead or at least happily stunned."

"You are sure?"

Guy squeezed her hand.

"Okay, I'll call Mr. Randall's studio tomorrow."

Guy hugged his daughter.

"Stan will sweep this mess in the morning."

He locked the bistro front and back door. Gloria made him unlock the door to the bar, so she could grab her treasured letter and envelope from the corkboard.

She drove home to her single-room apartment and flopped on the bed. In her excitement, she forgot to call her girlfriend.

"My dream will happen. I'm close."

She kicked her feet in the air and raised her hands over her head in delight. She taped the letter to her mirror. The paper gold crown hung over the edge.

"Nothing is going to mar my chances. I can be a star."

She remembered the poster advertising the Columbia Dancing Troupe. The male and female dancers were from the front string. A sense of foreboding suddenly filled Gloria. She shook her head.

"Don't get paranoid about a poster. The couple was in perfect ballet positions."

She sighed.

"There was tension. The female didn't look at her partner which seemed odd."

She rationalized that the photographer might not have been particularly good at staging the dancers.

"Still, I saw something."

3 Dancer Video Shoot

Rory Randall moved a client from his schedule to get Gloria Strand into his studio. She arrived promptly in her black tight outfit. She carried her new azure blue one-piece dance outfit in a dry-cleaning bag. Her ballet shoes were hand-dyed into a flesh-colored tone.

She met a good-looking man in black slacks and a white dress shirt. Gloria noticed his gold cufflinks. He appeared dressed for an expensive dinner engagement. The man looked like he stepped out of a magazine cover.

She swallowed. Her hand nervously extended in a handshake.

"Gloria Strand, how nice to meet you. Welcome to my studio. I'm Rory Randall, the owner. As you can see, we have everything here. There will be two camera operators. They work well together to capture your best angle and moves. They will do some long shots and closeups. I have your credit card information, and you won't be charged until you see and approve the videos. The dressing room is to the right. We'll let you do a warmup for five minutes, and then we begin. I have your music selections in my sound system."

Changing into her new tights outfit, she took one last look in the full-length mirror. The note explicitly stated bare feet for dancing in the first slow video. She liked dancing in bare feet. Her ballet shoes were brought along for good luck and the second fast video.

Gloria shrugged her shoulders so her hair would shake out. She wiggled her hands and did running steps. She was ready.

Entering the large studio space, she did a few leaps, turns, and dance routines. Her mind was a jumbled mess. She bit her lip and looked at the lighting. Rory appeared with two men. He introduced her.

"Take your position, Ms. Strand. When you are ready, give us a nod."

Gloria nodded and briefly closed her eyes to the first refrain. She liked the dark before she started to dance. The beginning notes swayed and soothed her. This was the slow portion of her dance routine. The song was about a woman and her power.

The dancing was expressive and slow at first. Her hand and feet moved in soft arcs as she tapped, twisted, and turned. She bowed low to the ground and did a low sit spin when the music began to fill the air. She moved upward from her spin into three flips and stopped fully poised with her leg in the back of her.

She turned, ran, and did three jumps and twirls in the death spirals. The legs rotated quickly down the length of the floor with arms reaching out and pulling toward her. Gloria dropped to her knees and into a split position.

Moving back up in a single foot position, she completed the dance in a final spiral coming to a slow stop facing the camera. She dropped to a bow and rose with her right hand in the air like a female warrior winning her lover's heart.

Rory had told her that he would make no comments until the end.

Gloria went to the table and took a drink of water. She laced her ballet shoes and tested the tightness. Satisfied, she positioned herself for the fast-paced dance.

The music started, and she danced quickly to the end, turned, and leaped in the air five times coming to a perfect one-second stop before she spun. There were larger arcs and turns while keeping perfect rhythm. Finally, the crescendo piece had Gloria leaping in the air with high and difficult steps. She gracefully stood, threw her head back, spun a final pirouette, and came to a quick stop. She deeply bowed.

Rory was amazed by the energy and strength this thin blue dancer showed. Her range and knowledge of ballet intrigued him. Her repertoire, choreography, and performance would win over the judges.

There were ballet turns, acrobats, deep arabesques, jete jumps, grand allegro, glissade, adage, and much more. The intricate dance executions and pointe work were gracefully completed. There were a few words he would use to describe Gloria Strand in his letter of recommendation.

"*Sheer superb ecstasy* is what I felt watching the woman perform."

Gloria came to him.

"Very impressive. The videos should be excellent. However, there might be a problem with the first video. The last quarter of your routine looks familiar. There was another dancer who dances the same steps. You may know this person."

Gloria was shocked.

"No one has seen me dance except once. There was one person who heard the song and my routine."

Rory excused his camera operators.

"Come into my office so we can talk."

Gloria thought Rory was mistaken. He showed her the last part of Geri's video.

Gloria was silent.

"Normally, I wouldn't interfere, but the judges will notice the similarity. The rules are the choreography must be original. Do you have another song and dance in your repertoire that we could film? I'm all right with doing a second video of your first dance routine. Then you can make your decision on which one to submit."

"I've been working on another routine in the early morning. I'm sure no one has seen it. There are a few bugs I need to work on to make the steps flow."

Rory checked his calendar.

"How about Thursday at eleven o'clock? We can take your photographs after the video."

Gloria nodded.

"Sure, I will be here. Should I say something to my friend?"

Rory stepped around his desk and sat on the edge.

"I wouldn't. If it were me, I would take my reaction and use everything I had to make this first routine beyond exceptional. Throw your passion into this one. Emphasize your moves. You want the judges to drop their pencils and notice the Gloria that I see. She's talented, brave, beautiful, and strong enough to dance with their troupe."

Gloria smiled, "I should blow them away."

Rory knew she could do just that.

"Sell your soul on the second try. You have nothing to lose. We'll see you on Thursday morning. Once you've decided, then I'll work on your items and have them ready by two o'clock on Friday. You should be able to personally deliver them to the company on the same day."

"Thank you, Mr. Randall."

Gloria left.

Rory called his girlfriend to move their dinner engagement. He made the mistake of telling her about a retake video for Gloria Strand.

He would work on the two videos this evening in case she wanted to keep the first video.

4 First Routine Video

Rory watched the second video of Gloria dancing. He knew this film was ten times better.

There was a light knock. He walked over, opened his door, and she stepped into his office.

"The second video is freer and more expressive. However, your first video is good, but it is what every candidate will submit. I see your intelligence and the ability to turn a selected piece of music into your special dance. Not many dancers can do this move so quickly. Which video do you want me to produce for your first routine? I know which one that I would select."

Gloria looked at her bag and knew the shoes were inside. The ballet shoes were off in the first routine. The judges wanted to know how she could dance with the modern contemporary steps.

It was time for a reality check. She watched the retake video. He was correct. She was freer with her movements, and there was happiness on her face. The choreography was better. The image she saw was herself dancing her dream to an absolute ten score.

Her photograph proofs were complete. She enjoyed Rory touching her, tilting her chin and arm to catch the proper lighting.

He told her as a kid, he photographed bugs, caterpillars, and butterflies. Next, he moved to squirrels and dogs. One day Rory decided to photograph a human being.

He selected a group of children at the playground. His choice was not a promising idea when he was confronted by angry mothers. Rory told them if he ever became a photographer with a studio, their children could have the top package of photographs for free.

From that point on, he became the neighborhood hero. Kids followed him everywhere wanting their picture taken. This was when his future career aspirations were exposed. Rory needed to buy a studio as soon as possible.

Gloria couldn't help but wonder how Rory found his true calling. His story was funny and sweet. She believed his story was told to help her relax and smile.

He stopped shooting her poses. Pulling the images from the computer to appear on a large screen, they both agreed on one photograph as the submittal to the judges. She bent way back, and her hair and face were lit. Her arms were bent as was one knee, and one leg was stretched straight out.

"You have two music pieces for the first dance in front of you. Let me know your decision."

Rory challenged the woman by shoving both videos toward her. She knew the music piece of her choice was important. Taking a piece of paper, she wrote the video numbers down. She flipped the paper over, so he wouldn't see the numbers until after she left.

Gloria grabbed her bag and exited Rory's studio.

He waited until she was gone and flipped the paper over. Rory grinned. She selected the correct video for her first routine. She chose the second take.

Her video photographer pushed the chair away from his desk. He didn't understand why he did this special change for Ms. Strand. He didn't like one of his clients being duped by another person.

He went to the video equipment room to refine the last film video and print her photographs. He would work until late, so the items would be ready. Satisfied with the videos and photos, he turned off the lights in the studio. He talked to himself.

"Gloria, you have remarkable skills. I hope you make the troupe. If not, I might know another troupe that would be interested. Your videos are amazing."

Rory went home. The next day, he wore his new suit with another dress shirt and the gold cufflinks because he was going out to dinner later.

She returned the next day and watched the completed videos again. The lighting and sound were perfect. Her dance routines were exceptional. The practice and training showed. Gloria was excited and pleased.

Suddenly, she noticed his new dark gray suit.

"You missed a tag on your arm." Gloria pointed. Rory was going to rip the tag off.

"No, I have tiny scissors. We sometimes repair our costumes."

He laughed while she touched his sleeve and snipped the threads holding the tag. She stood up and was close to Rory's face.

28

He smelled lilacs. The cologne made him look into her eyes. He caught his breath. Even though he saw her closeups, being in her presence sent his ticker to skip a few beats. She was younger, and her skin looked smooth.

"Thank you."

She blushed and stepped away. There was a change in his eyes when he looked at her.

"You are very welcome."

Rory took off his jacket and laid the clothing on his chair. He escorted her to the door and smiled when she exited his studio with the items in three black satin boxes. They fit neatly in one black bag.

He closed the door behind her.

"Gloria, you are going to make it. I see spectacular lights in your future. You won't be left standing in the dark for long. The energy flow around you when you dance sucked me into your fantasy world. There's a sparkle when you dance, and a special look called love. Your eyes gave you away. They tell the audience dancing is more important than anything in this world. If the judges miss that look, then you shouldn't dance in their company."

Fifteen minutes passed. Rory looked up to see his girlfriend standing in the doorway to his office. She was an hour early. His other work would have to wait until morning.

"You videotaped the blue dancer on two different days. What was her name? Ah, yes, Gloria Strand something. Isn't that a little extreme and extravagant with the cost of your time? I see she's picked up her film. Her older dusty car was driving out of your parking lot. She didn't look like she could afford your fees. Was she any good?"

Rory didn't appreciate her comments.

"Yes, and we needed to redo one of her tapes. It is my business to make sure what I send out of this studio is perfect. There was no additional cost to my client."

"Really, how nice."

She said the last words sarcastically. Rory grabbed his dress jacket with a black tie and escorted his girlfriend outside. She didn't care too much for being in his studio. Today he wanted her away from the building.

They were going to dinner at an expensive restaurant. He talked with the reservation girl over the phone after Gloria left. The reservation girl was a friend and told him about the executives from the Columbia Dancing Troupe were dining with the restaurant that evening.

Rory would introduce himself and drop the names of two female dancers he videotaped recently. He believed the two young women could use a shove in the right direction. He debated about giving them Geri Sullivan's name. He told himself to stay out of the two women's friendship.

When the judges read his letters of recommendation, they would remember his conversation. If the two women made the troupe, he could use their photographs for advertising his business. Rory knew how to play the game. He also wanted them to exceed beyond the troupe tour.

"Being a patron of the arts and a donor does help in the business world."

One of the dancers struck a nerve. She was hard to forget.

His girlfriend was not pleased by his absence with patrons of the arts.

"I thought we were going to be by ourselves this evening."

Rory sighed.

"This was necessary."

His girlfriend was not happy. Rory didn't know how to change the subject. They ate in silence.

The coffee and dessert arrived. His girlfriend toyed with the dessert. Rory put his fork down.

"Look, you must not interfere in my business."

The girlfriend stopped her swirl with the fork.

"Take me home. I have an early appointment."

Rory signaled the waiter.

5 Meeting & Final Lesson

Stan looked at the woman lying on the polished and clean wood countertop. He was glad there were no patrons in the building yet.

"Okay, what's eating at your brain, girl?"

"I'm not a girl anymore."

Gloria took a bite out of the cherry she stole from the glasses of fruit he was assembling.

"I have eyes and see that you have grown. Stop eating all the cherries. Your teeth will turn red. Then you will look like an old vampire in a movie I watched."

She grabbed another one and held the red sphere between her teeth. He moved the glass to the other end. Gloria swallowed the fruit.

"Fruit is good for you. It's the food coloring that's the problem. The word eating is wrong. Spinning works better. My brain is rushing around and around like a cement mixer. I'm exhausted from waiting for a response. The dance troupe judges are taking their time. The competition must be heavy."

Stan finished with the last glass of condiments. He washed his hands and put the paper towel in the garbage. Small bud vases of lilacs sat on the tables.

Stan looked at her small frame, moved the stool out of his way, and pulled himself up onto the counter. He sat near her head of ponytailed curls. She was in socks that matched her hair tie. Today she wore gold. His pretty friend was unhappy.

"We've known each other too long for you to kid me. Talk to your older and wiser friend."

The dancer resigned herself to tell her tale. Gloria sat cross-legged, so she could talk easier. He noticed there was a small sprig of lilac on the bar. Stan put the stem under her hair tie.

"The flower was wanting to be in your curls. What gives, Gloria?"

Stan waited. He saw her distress.

"Jordan Sullivan is in town. He's been here a week. I ran into him outside the ice cream store on Fifth Avenue by chance. We talked briefly. He will be returning to the state of Washington. He's working on a ferry that travels to Friday's Harbor. He owns a small boat there. He wanted to know if I would go back with him. I told him that I couldn't. He was pissed that I applied to the dance troupe. That's when I left."

Stan got down off the top and helped Gloria to a tall stool. He turned the stool toward him.

"Does your old man know?"

"No, and not one person in this building is going to tell him."

Gloria stared at Stan waiting for his reply.

"I won't tell him, but you should."

Gloria shook her head negatively.

Stan knew she was being stubborn. Women could get that way fast. He ran into brick walls before, and they were breakable. Now the New York style of women was different. He knew their walls contained rebar a foot thick.

"The accident you were involved in at age eighteen was bad. Jordan was driving. You were hurt. He wasn't. A year of your life disappeared. It took that long to get your dancing abilities back. Your father won't ever forgive him, and you shouldn't either. Jordan's pissed that you applied to the dance troupe. Well, tell him to take a hike and go back to Washington. Dancing and your life are none of his business."

Gloria was glad Stan was in the bistro today. She needed a friend to listen to her. She couldn't talk to Geri about her strange brother.

"Yeah, I'm not stupid. He doesn't get the true me and never will. I just needed affirmation from a friend that I should stay on my track."

Stan touched her shoulder and was going to go back into the kitchen.

"There is one more thing. Geri copied my song and used the last part of my routine for her first video. Rory, my photographer, caught the duplicate part and allowed me to change my song and dance with a retake."

Stan was disturbed by her second piece of news.

"Geri has always imitated your dance moves. The photographer was nice."

"I know she has but the troupe letter was specific about originality. This job was important to me, and the judges would be wise."

Stan touched her face.

"This face belongs to someone I love, and I'm glad the woman chose wisdom to guide her future. You did the retake."

He kissed her forehead.

"Thanks for picking up the lilacs from the Henderson Florist. They missed your congratulation party and knew you liked lilacs."

"These white lilacs are heavenly."

"That is not all. The pizza people gave your dad twenty-five frozen pizzas. We received two hams from the Andrews, and the Devan's gave us four strings of homemade sausages with buns. People have been happy for you and your dad. The cards and money have come in. There are five hundred more dollars. He's personally thanked them."

"I'm pleased they want to support us on my journey. When I'm famous, we'll get other people tickets."

Gloria hugged Stan and left him to go to her dancing lesson.

This was her last lesson with Pierre Denton. They were working on a backward lift to his shoulder, a spin, and a lift-off. He was teaching her how to dance with a male partner. She was learning at a fast pace, so she would be ready for the Columbia Dancing Troupe. She watched videos of their shows, and she and her teacher tried the dance steps together.

Pierre was full of praise regarding her skills as a ballet dancer and gymnast. Her lightweight body made it easier for him to carry her through their jump routines.

He told her she would be ready for a partner or doubles dancing. In the future, whenever she was given the opportunity, she should dance with the male dancers. Each person developed their style even though the moves might be the same.

Gloria was surprised to see a different male dancer with Pierre.

"This is Dillon Andrews. He will substitute for me for our routine. This way my previous words will make sense to you. Then, I'll work with you on the final jump."

"All right," commented Gloria.

"By the way, he is a former student of mine and has been with a small local ballet company as a substitute dancer for the past year."

After her program with Dillon, she waved him goodbye.

"Well, tell me the difference," asked Pierre.

Gloria wiped her face on a towel.

"He was faster, lifted me higher, and he kept the beat. His footwork was very solid."

"Dillon uses his powerful muscles better than I do. Once a difficult jump is over, he softly moves your body. The program I saw showed a controlled beauty by both human forms."

Gloria finished her class and received her certificate.

"Pierre, this has been fun, but I must hurry to work. I appreciated the opportunity of dancing with Mr. Andrews. We will dance again in the future. I'll keep you up to date on whether I'm selected."

Gloria went home to wait another day. Tomorrow was Friday, and she began to worry. Friday was the cutoff. The hours on the clock slowly rotated around.

There was no phone call from the agent from the Columbia Dancing Troupe.

Self-doubt was rolling in. She felt anxious and depressed. She knew the other dance candidates were holding their breaths. Gloria took her medicine before bedtime and went to bed.

6 Phone Call

Friday at 9:30 in the morning Gloria pulled over to the curb two blocks from the bakery and her father's bistro to answer her phone. She wasn't going to the dance studio today because of a much-needed hair appointment for a trim and wash.

The rain started pattering loudly against her windshield. The large drops might wash the city dirt away. She turned on her windshield wipers to clear the view. The wiper squeaked loudly, and the rubber separated off the metal. The broken rubber flew off to land somewhere else. She quickly turned the device off.

Gloria spoke to the troupe agent and dug her pen and paper out of her gym bag. She wrote the address and suite number down. The agent gave her the name of the building and the floor number.

The Columbia Dancing Troupe's receptionist would take her to the conference room for her last face-to-face interview with the manager, Mr. Lang. The agent told her they were extremely impressed with her videos. The agent corrected herself.

"They loved both routines. Your videos were solid and professional. You have a gift."

Gloria told the agent she was excited and would meet the manager of the dancing troupe on Monday at one in the afternoon.

She sat in her car stunned. The broken wiper didn't matter.

Suddenly, she dug out quarters for the meter and went outside in the rain. After depositing two dollars in coins, she ran to her father's bistro and burst through the door.

Her father came out from behind the coffee area and held out his arms. Gloria fell into his soft and comfortable body. Guy Strand knew she made the final interview.

"Congratulations to my girl!"

She wiped the tears from her eyes.

"I'll be back. My hair appointment is like right now. Then I'm going to buy a new suit, blouse, shoes, and a briefcase. Oh, have Stan get me new wipers. Mine broke or at least one did, and parts fell off."

Her father let his daughter go, and he looked at Stan who said, "I didn't get a hug."

Guy grinned. It was not like Gloria to forget.

"Gloria told us she would be back. I'm going to call the man about getting the neon dancer sign ordered. She's going to be our star."

Guy threw a twenty-dollar bill on the counter. Stan pocketed the money.

"I'll get the wipers on my way home."

Stan poured them each a cup of coffee. They would both need fifteen minutes for their excitement to die down. They knew Gloria's thrill ride would take longer.

Gloria was exceptionally quiet until her hairdresser stopped. She didn't want to have crooked hair. When she told her hairstylist, she knew the gossip would go ten miles around the area. All her father's friends would know as well.

Driving to the large department store, she took her time selecting a basic black suit, white silk blouse, black heels, and a black leather briefcase. She finished her look with an expensive blue scarf and gold chain. At the last minute, she bought a gold bracelet and put the charge on her credit card. Her father's check for her bistro work would cover the cost of the bracelet.

Gloria sat down in a quiet restaurant booth inside the department store with her salad and a vanilla latte. She took her phone out and started calling Geri Sullivan. It was three o'clock in the afternoon. She hung up.

"What if she didn't make the troupe?"

Gloria knew five o'clock was the cutoff of when the dance troupe agent would call the final cut of dancers for their interview.

A man walked over. Gloria looked up to see Rory Randall. He was carrying a plate with a roast beef sandwich and fruit salad. She motioned for him to sit down. He could tell by the look in her eyes and the bags of expensive clothing that she made the final cut. He sat down.

"I like to eat here when they have roast beef. The chef slow cooks the meat and spices everything perfectly. Then he adds homemade horseradish sauce. I like good food. You made the final interview because there is this silly and incredibly happy look on your face."

Gloria nodded.

"I am so incredibly happy for you. You do know the interview will go smoothly. After seeing you dance, I was hooked."

Gloria knew the interview was an introduction only and for the added Human Resource paperwork involved. Arrangements and training schedules would also be handed out. The troupe would be training in the city for the next three weeks before they left on their tour.

"How does it feel to be this close to stardom?"

She swallowed her salad bite.

"Blissful and anxious to begin. My dreams have started to come true. My father and his friends believed in me, Mr. Randall," replied Gloria.

"You can call me Rory. Anyone who snips a tag off a piece of my clothing is considered a friend. From now on, we are good friends."

"Tell me why you were hooked on dancing?" asked Gloria.

"Oh, my mother took me to the ballet. I'm an old hand at understanding the footwork of a grand plie from a demi-plie. She would point out the various jumps and steps. I know your training takes years and years of dedication. I admire a person who works hard. There's the talent thing. You worked harder than most to make the grade."

They talked together for an hour before Rory left her. He paid for her check and two glasses of white wine.

Gloria and Rory parted ways at the elevator, and she walked to her car in the parking lot on the third floor. Putting her packages in the trunk, she stepped over to the wall edge and looked at the city of New York.

People were bustling below, and cars were honking their horns. The place was noisy. She could smell restaurants firing up their fryers for the evening. French fries, beef tacos, and Asian chicken were cooking. The Korean restaurant smelled of spicy pork. The Fish House was heating raw shrimp in their huge pans. A coffee shop was cooking coffee beans to place in foiled bags for sale. The smell was a heavy blend of Asian-American fusion.

"Earthy and heavenly with a little soot thrown in. A very New York feeling kind of place."

The streetlights hadn't yet turned on. She glanced at her watch. The time showed four-thirty.

Gloria went back to her car and called her father to let him know when she would arrive home late.

Halfway home, a call came across her phone while she was on the expressway. The time was four forty-five. The call was from Geri.

Gloria waited until she was at her father's back parking lot. She called her friend. Geri did make the troupe, and the next interview was scheduled later than Gloria's.

Her friend didn't seem to notice she was called last. Gloria went inside with her packages. She felt good that she hadn't accused her friend of cheating. Her father helped her carry the shopping bags upstairs.

She told him about meeting the photographer at the restaurant and briefly mentioned talking with Geri.

Her father frowned. Normally, she was excited about Geri. He knew something was off between the two women. He wondered if Stan knew what was wrong.

"I'll get Stan to fix your wipers and wash your car."

Guy left Gloria to unpack her garments and when she was done, she stared at herself in the full-length mirror. Leaning against the dance barre, she knew that she didn't look any different.

She changed into a pretty cotton short sundress over a fitted undergarment with attached panties. This evening was a catered casual affair courtesy of her father with barbeque sandwiches, chips, pickles, and cookies. The Gloria fans would be there.

"You better get used to being in the spotlight. The audience will be sitting in the dark waiting for you to appear. The shows will be spectacular."

Gloria did a deep bow to her imaginary audience and smiled. The panties covered any twirl. She knew how to dance, and she was ready for the scheduled shows. Reaching the top was what she wanted.

"No looking back."

She fingered an old picture of herself at age six in a leotard outfit with a tutu. The photograph was black and white. She remembered there were yellow stars against a blue background with red netting.

"A costume for the Fourth of July."

The photo was taken when she and her mother still lived with her father. She sighed. The day was hot, and they went to the park to watch a parade. She could only remember happy times. Gloria never knew why her parents parted. Her father mentioned a rift.

Written across the photo in her mother's handwriting were the words, *Reach for the stars, my baby, spread your wings and fly en l'air!*

She placed the twig of white lilac next to the picture frame.

"Love you, momma."

Gloria went downstairs to the party.

7 Business Day

Gloria was fifteen minutes early for her dance troupe appointment and sat in the waiting room. The building was the same one with the dance poster. The gray building held the troupe's executive offices.

She was surprised to see Dillon Andrews come through the door close to the receptionist. He carried a large box and a garment bag. His eyes lit up when he saw her.

"Hi, Gloria Strand. We meet again. The pleasure is all mine. What time did the agent call you?"

"Hello, Dillon. I think nine-thirty."

Mr. Andrews chuckled delightedly.

"Beat you. My session was at nine o'clock. It looks like we will get to dance together in the future. I'm glad you remembered my name. I must have made an impact."

Gloria didn't know what to say to him other than, "I look forward to your amazing control."

The receptionist called her name.

Dillon winked.

"Good luck, pretty dancer, see you soon at rehearsal."

Gloria followed the receptionist and met her new boss, Markus Lang.

Mr. Lang congratulated her on meeting all their requirements and welcomed her to the dance troupe. She filled out the extra paperwork while he explained the history of the company. He handed her the rehearsal schedule and showed her the map with the building location. She noted the building was in a large grouping of warehouses.

Another booklet contained the tour cities, dance locations, hotels, busing, and airline arrangements. The second packet was the company emergency phone numbers.

Next, she was taken to a room where a woman measured her body and feet size. She was handed her temporary practice shoes and plain dance garments in her size. The tour costumes and special ballet shoes would be sewn and handed to them after the rehearsals were completed in three weeks.

The entire interview and process took exactly fifty minutes. She walked out the door near the receptionist with her box and garment bag.

Gloria put her items in the car and drove to her old dance place close to home. She changed out of the new suit and put her black tights and comfortable top on. This time she wore her ballet shoes and decided to change her routine.

A video she saw of a famous dancer gave her a new idea. Gloria wanted to see if she could master the steps and put her spin on them.

Stopping and starting once a series was down pat in her memory, she moved to the second set. She worked for over four hours and finally stopped. Gloria wrote herself a note to ask Stan for his video camera. She would record the routine and save it on her computer. There was a second program she wanted to try.

"It's always good to have four complete programs in your brain just in case things fail down the road."

She looked at her laptop computer.

"Hello, brain."

Geri called her and complained that she didn't like her green costume color from the dancing troupe. Gloria hadn't even checked her garment bag. She vaguely remembered green and royal blue.

"Didn't you read the dancer lineup?" asked Geri exasperatedly.

"No, I figured that all the stuff in my box and garment bag could wait until this weekend. My brain was a little fried after the interview this morning. Mr. Lang talked amazingly fast. I went to my dance building to unwind and get the kinks out."

"Geesh, I am so screwed. They put me in the bottom group of dancers. I'll be in the back row, not the middle. I don't understand. My videos were great. I even used a tiny part of your routine. We both liked the same song."

Gloria didn't know how to stop her friend's disappointment regarding her placement. Her unhappiness with her friend and her naïve revelation about copying part of her routine surprised her. Geri didn't see anything wrong with what she had done.

"About your using the same song and copying part of my routine, you shouldn't have. The troupe's letter said the work must be original choreography. The judges aren't stupid. I quickly changed my first video routine and song."

"You are mad at me? I can't believe this would be a problem. I always copy your dances. I don't think they would have caught the tiny piece. Randall told you, didn't he?"

Gloria shook her head. She wasn't mentioning the photographer's role. He wasn't the one responsible.

"Well, don't even do tiny in the future. We're professionals now. I expect you to grow up."

Geri was quiet.

"Now I'm more depressed. You did work hard to submit a different routine? I didn't realize it. Maybe I should give this dance stuff up."

Gloria was expected to cheer her friend out of the doldrums. Looking back, she had been doing exactly the sympathetic listener route for Geri her whole life. She knew Geri couldn't talk to her parents or brother.

"Don't give up. We should be happy. A week ago, we didn't know if we made the troupe. We are in the top ten chosen from the city. You should be proud. I am immensely proud to have made the troupe. Stan, my dad, and his pub patrons believed in us. You can't quit. They love to watch us dance."

Geri simmered down.

"All right. I'm sorry. Did you see anyone you knew when you went to the interview?"

Gloria didn't want to mention Mr. Andrews but was now forced to confess.

"I did run into someone I met at Pierre's last class. He was a former student, and we were doing partner routines. His name is Dillon Andrews. I partnered with him for one routine. He has been an alternate for a local ballet company for a year in the city."

"So, the guy is good and experienced."

Gloria knew she brightened her friend's day by changing the focus from dancing to men.

"Very good indeed."

Geri wanted to know if she could tell her more information regarding the young man.

"I don't have anymore, but you should be able to talk to him at our first rehearsal."

Geri became a different person and was talking a true-blue streak about men. Her friend was going to enjoy rehearsals. She listened but Gloria needed to drive home and take a hot shower.

"We can talk later. I'm bushed."

Geri finally ended the call.

Curious, Gloria went to her car and opened the troupe garment bag. Her rehearsal costume was green with large royal blue and gold designs intertwined in stripes down the costume. Mostly, the color was royal blue. She opened the cardboard box and found the color coding for their positions on the floor with the dance company.

A surprised look spread over her face. Her costume was with the middle dancers. The front row was where the more experienced dancers stood. They held their positions from the previous year and wore total royal blue with tiny touches of gold braid. She looked at the other garment in the bag. There was a royal blue jacket with an emblem. Everyone in the troupe would get the same jacket. She touched the troupe company logo.

Gloria made the top cut in the middle row. She would be ahead of her friend. Instantly, she knew Dillon would be in her row. He was an excellent performer. She smiled remembering how he lifted her.

"I wonder what my future will hold in store. The troupe did really like my first video. I'm glad Rory let me retake the video. Without the retake, I might be in the back row or not at all. Mr. Randall might have changed my life."

Her mind was trying to think of a way to repay him.

"Rory was nice and a real pro. Cute doesn't come close to good-looking, interesting, and intelligent. Let's heap on the friend part."

Gloria wanted a future beyond dancing. Suddenly she understood dancing wasn't the ultimate path. There was a lot more.

She tried her new wipers. They worked.

"Perfect."

Her car was shiny clean, and the engine sounded better.

"Stan must have changed the oil, filter, and done a good tune-up."

Gloria relaxed. She was all right and safe from poverty.

"Let's not forget a wreck from an older vehicle."

She was pleased, "I have a job and money."

8 Dance Troupe

The middle dancers were six performers alternating from male to female. Their manager, Markus Lang, motioned for Dillon and Gloria to come forward. He pointed to the side of the room and the other four dancers moved and stood on the sidelines.

"We do couples dancing and sometimes need to give the first string of dancers a break. Whoever performs the best will become the alternate couple. Dillon and Gloria will perform first. Tell the sound man your song selection and show me your stuff."

Markus settled in a chair. Gloria and Dillon talked about their choices. He wanted to perform the dance they did at Pierre's studio. She wanted to venture higher and asked if he knew a specific dance. He did know and danced recently with his ballet company. She told him she might need a little of his guidance.

"No problem. I've danced with you, and I do know how you move. Let my experience help us."

He gave the sound man their selection, and the two dancers went to their positions. There was only a slight hesitation by Gloria on one jump. Dillon gave her a minute by doing a slight bow to her. They performed the complicated jump and ended their routine.

Their manager was standing and clapping.

"Bravo, a smart move in selecting Yavne's dance routine. He and Ms. Karon were superb. You two have done your homework. You showed me that you can match an important beat. The beat is one called success. Next couple."

At the end of their morning, Dillon and Gloria were chosen as the double alternates. They were excused for the rest of the afternoon. The two went to celebrate lunch at the nearest restaurant.

The last row of dancers was brought into the studio with the two older alternate dancers from the front row. The alternates were there to help lead the young singers in the introduction dance.

Geri knew the steps of their routine. However, the ending changed in that they would form a circle and do leaps once around. The middle row dancers joined them.

Geri didn't like one of the alternate women dancers. The alternate was rude. She argued with her in the bathroom regarding Geri's jump. Geri swore under her breath and whispered to herself.

"Stuff it, you mean old battle-ax."

The woman overheard her and pushed Geri against the wall. Geri pushed back. Another dancer intervened.

Geri yelled, "You're going to fall flat on your face someday because you jump wrong. I went to a better school than you did. You are dancing in the old school way. I know jumps. They were the redeeming feature that helped put me into this job."

"The school you went to taught you how to fudge your steps," taunted the woman.

Geri looked meanly back at the woman.

Unfortunately, she was placed next to the woman in the final circle of leaps. Geri looked at the dancers in the circle and realized Dillon and Gloria were missing. She came to a full stop when the alternate was leaping into the air.

The alternate ran into her. The two women crashed. Geri was the first one to try to stand. She limped a little.

"I think I have a slight sprain."

The alternate didn't move, and an ambulance was called disrupting the day's practice session. The troupe thought the alternate dancer was faking her injury.

In the end, Geri did have a slight sprain and wouldn't dance until after the next rehearsal. The alternate was out of the tour due to a broken leg. This changed the back-row dancer's attitudes.

When Geri came back to the troupe, the last string wouldn't talk to her.

"It was an accident. I was looking for Dillon and Gloria. Didn't anyone notice they were missing?"

No one answered back. One of the young male dancers came forward.

"You don't need to rub things in our faces. We just want to forget the incident."

Geri was frustrated, "I'm a New Yorker. We talk this way when people rattle our cage. Besides, I told her she didn't know how to jump. Not only did she not know how to jump, but her landing was the worst."

She saw Dillon and Gloria arrive back at the studio. They were beaming and told her about their new positions. Geri hugged them both. Her day was now complete.

"The old battle-ax is gone, and my ballet friends have returned."

Geri left early because the practice was canceled for the day. She drove to Rory Randall's studio to pick up her large photograph for her dad's office. She was disappointed only Rory's assistant was in the building's office. Geri wondered if Rory was upset with her about copying Gloria's dance stuff. She figured the two films did show him the truth.

"I shouldn't have been so desperate to win. Too late for remorse. My best friend almost disappeared from my life. I'll be a better friend in the future."

The assistant showed her the photograph. Geri knew her father would be pleased. She didn't know this would be her last professional photograph.

9 Dancing with Dan

One of the first row's lead male dancers was sent to the hospital after having contracted measles. The manager asked if everyone else ever had measles. They did and were safe. He was joyful.

Dillon was moved from the middle row to the first row. Because he was the next dancer in the position, the other dancers were not jealous. They believed Dillon belonged in the front.

A man from the back row was moved into Dillon's old position. Gloria was upset because she believed she would move to the next position with Dillon. She heard some grumblings from the women dancers that this company pushed the males to the top.

The women were sympathetic in the locker room that now Gloria would be doubled with Dan Gibbons. They told her to be prepared because Dan wasn't as good as Dillon.

"Footwork problems," mentioned a dancer.

The next day Gloria found out what the women dancers meant. He missed some steps in the routine. The manager was not pleased and told Dan to study the routine or get moved to the back row permanently.

Gloria was untying her ballet shoes when Dan approached her.

"Our manager doesn't like me because I'm gay."

"Do you suppose he didn't see three missed footsteps in your routine? I saw them. The man is smart, and you would be better off doing what he asks instead of worrying about your sex life."

He blushed.

"My concentration is a little off. I did miss the steps. My friend wants me to quit the show and move to Casper, Wyoming. I've been there and don't want to go back even for a vacation. The grass and buffalo make me ill. I like all the concrete in this city. The dogs aren't woolly mammoths."

"Why would he want you to quit? We are making good money dancing with this troupe. You do have talent but need to concentrate more."

Geri came over and entered the discussion.

"Yes, and we worked hard to get into this troupe. Well, some of us did."

Geri looked at Gloria.

"I would drop this male friend who wants you to quit. It seems to me that he doesn't want you to have all this freedom, sweat, and agony," volunteered Geri.

"I've been so busy trying to practice that I haven't gone out with the others at night. I need nightlife, and I'm miserable," complained Dan.

Geri grabbed his arm, "Well, I know how to fix your situation, Mr. Gibbons."

"Call me Dan."

"All right. Some of the dancers from the first row invited me to go along with them. We can squeeze you into the van. Cheer up. Miserable people belong in opera, not ballet."

Dan brightened and forgot about his friend, Johnny Zander.

"I like you, Geri."

As they were leaving, Gloria reminded Dan that she expected him to appear at nine o'clock in the morning to go over their dance routine.

The next day Dan and Geri showed up at the troupe's dance studio. Geri decided she could help him with one jump and turn. After practice, they were surprised to see a man standing near the doorway. Gloria walked into the studio from the opposite direction. They wondered how he got through security.

Dan introduced Johnny to the two women.

Johnny commented that he would remember their names. All he needed to do was think of two G-strings.

Dan was horrified and quickly escorted his friend outside.

Geri was mad.

"The little creep named Johnny is nasty. We need to convince Dan more than ever to drop the lizard before his career is in jeopardy. Sexual maniac on the loose. Mr. Zander is not welcome to any of our parties."

"I agree with you," said Gloria. "The comment was not appreciated nor was it funny. We don't even look like hookers, and that was his implication."

"Yeah, I don't see any dance poles or red lights in this place to set the creep off. Nor are our costumes out of line. Maybe he doesn't like New Yorker women and lumps them in one category."

Gloria put her ballet shoes next to her bag.

"I don't believe the man likes any humans, male or female in New York or Wyoming. An alien planet would be a better place for him to exist."

"Yeah, park him on an exo-planet thirteen thousand light-years away would be my choice. How far away is Mars, Pluto, or Uranus? I can't remember the other planet names. Maybe the transport ship could permanently break down."

Gloria thought about the exo-planet and spoke.

"We need to stay away from him. He gave me the willies just looking at him. Danger signs were flashing in my female brain."

Geri made sure the outer door was closed and the lock clicked.

"There was something about the man that seemed odd. The willies you felt were from the way the man looked at us. He reminded me of the headless rider. I also hated the weird metal on his face. I know lots of gay men, and they don't act or look the way this guy does. Too many nose rings are creepy."

"I appreciate your helping today. Dan looked much better in the last routine."

Geri grabbed her gym bag, and the two dancers left the room for the next couple to practice in the allotted time slot.

10 The Drug Dancer

A female dancer from the first row was in the bathroom. Geri overheard the dancer talk to another woman about a packet and the required payment. She didn't think any more about the conversation.

"Packets of onions or did they say opiates? I don't know. I hate both. You won't see me buying either one."

This was the week when all the dancers would work together. They were booked into a hotel, so the dancers could spend more time on their routines if needed. There were five sets of routines they memorized and their doubles routine. Their manager decided to add an eighth routine using the double dancers only from the first and middle rows.

The five sets were completed, and the back-row dancers were dismissed. The doubles dancers went to the small auditorium to watch a video of the movement their manager wanted them to master. Geri came along to learn. Gloria sat with Geri, Dillon, and Dan.

"Do people buy onions here?" asked Geri.

Dan told Geri to be quiet. Gloria took out her computer and was going to tape the show. Dillon took out his computer as well.

Both Geri and Dan were to print the names of the steps, and they decided to compare their notes and videos at a local coffee shop.

While in the coffee shop, they corrected their notes, and Dan's was the best video. He copied the two files and sent them to each person's email.

They went back to Dan's hotel room and practiced the routine. The couch and chair were shoved out of the way. They couldn't do the jumps but said the jump name aloud.

By ten o'clock in the evening, they received a knock from the company administrative person who handed them their time slot in the gym area to practice with their partners.

Gloria noticed she was partnered with Dillon.

"Shouldn't I be dancing with Dan?" questioned Gloria.

The administrative person told them about a female dancer from the front row who was arrested for selling drugs. She would not be coming back to the tour. Instead of using the alternate who also was arrested, the dancers were moved. Gloria would spend the rest of the tour dancing with Dillon in the front row.

Dillon's eyes gleamed a little too much when Gloria looked at him. He might be a handful. She heard rumors about him.

Geri would move from the back row to the middle row and would be dancing with Dan. The manager felt Geri was a better match for Dan.

Geri jumped up and down in her excitement.

"I'm in the middle row. Thank you so much. I can't believe that I made it to the second line. They were talking about opiates, not onions."

The three dancers stopped and looked at Geri.

"They were in the bathroom. I didn't think I overheard correctly."

Gloria hugged her as did Dillon.

"I should have asked you about the onion comment," offered Gloria.

Dan frowned and then extended his hand to Geri.

"Oh, for heaven's sake, come here."

Geri opened her arms, and Dan embraced her and blushed.

The other dancers would know in the morning when they found the gym assignments under their door. Their new costumes would be available for the Miami show. The men said goodnight.

Gloria left with Geri.

"I should be going back to my room," said Gloria.

Geri finally came down from her cloud nine thrill moment.

"Drat, now I have to dance with Dan for the rest of the tour."

Gloria chuckled. It served her right.

"Better you than me. The costume colors are better. At least your feet are smaller than mine. Dan might do better with a female with shorter feet."

"The only problem now is my boobs. I might need to wear a compression top to shrink them."

Gloria burst out in tears of laughter. She opened her door. Walking over to her clothing bag, she pulled out a flesh-toned top.

"Here, I brought an extra one."

Geri took the top.

Gloria said, "Goodnight. Maybe the frog will turn into a prince of a dancer."

"Get out!"

Geri picked up a pillow and threw it at Gloria before she left.

Gloria sat on her bed in the hotel room. She put the pillow on the chair.

"My costume will be royal blue."

She sent a text to Rory.

"I'm going to be a blue dancer."

Gloria did a bold move. She finished typing some words and hesitated. "I shouldn't, but it is time to be brave."

Wish you were here.

She sent a second text to her father and Stan. Her dad sent her an emoji-type grin and a picture of their neon blue dancer sign. There wasn't a return text from Rory.

She sighed. The rest of the dancers' week was calm. The dance routines were working, and the kinks were gone. The women felt confident in going forward.

Markus was happy with the turn of events.

He decided not to bring in the two alternates that were on his list. He hoped to save the company six hundred thousand dollars plus the same amount for the couple that dropped out. The audience only wanted to see feet flying in the air and great music. They never counted the number of dancers.

Markus watched the friendships grow between the dancers. Dan was welcomed into the flock. On their nights off, Dan partied with some of the front-row dancers. He was too busy to visit his friend Johnny.

Dan made up excuses that the training was what kept him occupied.

Geri sometimes went to parties. Gloria stayed in the hotel room hoping for a phone call.

The time arrived for their first performance. The dancers were ready for the show in Atlantic City.

Their gear was packed in New York City, and they traveled by two buses to the hotel and casino.

The destination signs on the front of the busses carried the city name. The back of the bus windows held a transparent sign with the company's troupe name. They would use one company's buses for the entire tour.

The dance group was quiet during the bus ride to Atlantic City. Some of the dancers were playing cards and others were reading or sleeping. Geri and Gloria sat together.

"Scared," asked Geri.

Gloria looked at her friend.

"Scared Silly."

"My dad gave me some money to gamble. I don't like to gamble."

Gloria took her jacket out of her bag and slipped her arms inside.

"Do you want your jacket? We can try the quarter machines at the casino. They might be fun."

"Yes, the bus is a little cool. Okay to the quarter machines."

Gloria found Geri's jacket. She settled down with her book reader. Geri fell asleep.

There was a large stage where they would perform on Saturday and Sunday nights. The gymnasium for practice was across the street from the casino.

Mr. Lang was on the other bus with the costumes and equipment. He required peace, distance from his energetic dancers, and quiet. He was pleased they were finally on the road

11 Atlantic City

Gloria, Dillon, Geri, Dan, and the front row dancers named Bella and Clark Reine headed for the beach when they arrived at their Atlantic City hotel on Friday.

They all wore their casual tights and royal blue logo jackets. Dillon carried his computer and bag with him. He was going to record and watch a copy of their routine at a table close by the lifeguard stand.

Instead of sitting at the table, they all took their shoes off and walked in the water. Dillon noticed the children playing in the sand and their tired-looking parents.

"I've got an idea. Why don't we do a quarter of the dance for our little friends?"

Clark said, "I don't think we should. Our contract discourages spur-of-the-moment dancing. Every scene is set up by management. Besides, these people aren't going to pay us."

Bella jabbed Clark in the stomach. He gave her a strange look. Dillon intervened.

"I've read a little bit about the law. We can dance except we need to shake things up. Let's be looser and more modern. In other words, it's not technically the same dance as the troupe show."

Gloria and Geri nodded. They could crazily dance. They told them they improvised all the time at Gloria's Bistro on the wood countertop. The two women showed them the exaggerated steps and a little shimmy of their bootie.

"Okay, a little less on the bootie," pleaded Dan.
Bella stood quietly.

"No, the women should go for it," urged Clark.

Dillon noticed the children stopped shoveling sand and were watching them. Out of the corner of his eye, he saw a news truck.

"I'll bet you fifty dollars we make the news tonight."

The other dancers saw the white van with gear on the top.

Clark wanted to get the news people.

Dillon shook his head. "We do this my way and dance half the song. We're just out-of-town dancers having fun. That should give them enough time to get their cameras ready."

They deposited their jackets in the sand with their shoes. Dillon restarted his computer and put his jacket on the whitewashed wood after clicking the sound button for the dance routine.

The parents looked up when they heard the music and watched the dancers perform. They were halfway through the dance when they saw the news media running toward them.

"Let's finish the routine and ramp it up!"

The sand was flying as they twirled and strutted their stuff. The women took their headbands off and let their hair swing to the beat. Their shoulders were loose and rocking. The men mimicked the women who knew the latest crazy modern moves better.

The news media camera was rolling. The dance was completed, and the beach dancers bowed low to the children who were jumping up and down and trying some of their dance moves.

The parents came over to thank them. The news media people talked with all of them and got their names. They signed a quick-release form, so the news could play a piece of their video that evening.

Picking up their dance jackets and shoes, the dancers went to their rooms to meet later for dinner.

Their manager was watching the news when he saw his dancers performing near the water. He saw how they danced. The motion was different.

He liked what he saw. The six dancers improved the troupe's routine. His phone rang, and the tickets were sold out for Saturday night's performance. Sunday night was seventy-five percent booked and rising.

Markus quickly dressed and went to the elevator to get to the restaurant on the seventh floor. He saw the group of dancers and went over to their table.

Dillon saw him first.

"Oh, oh, our boss is coming our way."

Dillon, Dan, and Clark stood up to greet him.

"Sit down, sit down, men," said Markus.

"I've reserved the smaller gym for you, six dancers. Meet me there at nine o'clock in the morning. We're going to change the couples' dance. Shake the dance out as you did on the beach, and then we'll train the other couples. We never get the young crowd in our shows. Your dancing is going to change our audience and increase the numbers."

Markus left the group to eat their steak dinner. When the group was done eating, they sat and talked about their day.

Dan noticed Johnny standing in the doorway watching the group have an enjoyable time. Johnny also saw the news and was angry. He arrived at the hotel early, and there was no Dan to be found.

"Excuse me, let me introduce you to my friends."

Dan introduced everyone who was at their table, and then the two men left.

Geri was the first to speak. "That's the second time I've met the man. He's still a creep. How far away is Jupiter? We can buy him a ticket to the lightning show. Jupiter has lightning, I think."

Gloria agreed with the ticket idea.

Dillon interjected, "Jupiter has high altitude lightning storms plus a few cyclones. I would call the Zander person shifty and very abrupt. He must not like dancers."

Geri commented, "Neither human, animal, nor insect."

12 Rory's Appearance

After the Saturday night show, the dancers changed out of their show costumes and were planning on gambling for the evening.

They were walking down the hallway to their room to stow their gear when Gloria saw Rory near her door. He turned and saw her coming.

She motioned to Dillon that she would meet with the others later.

"I can wait."

She shook her head and shoved him toward his room. Dillon didn't look happy. He knew Rory was Gloria and Geri's photographer. The man was too good-looking and successful.

"I don't trust him," whispered Dillon.

Gloria whispered back.

"I do. Now go."

Dillon walked away.

She stopped in front of Rory and excitedly gave him a quick hug. She was happy to see him. He held her a little longer than necessary in his arms.

"How nice to see you in Atlantic City? Are you staying at our hotel?"

Rory released her.

"Gloria, you look great. I was in New Jersey picking up new lights for my studio when I saw your group dancing in the sand on the news. I would know your elegant legs and feet anywhere. Immediately, I called the troupe's website number and purchased tickets for your show tonight. I'm glad that I did. The show was amazing. My surprise was watching you start the show as part of the Pas de deux."

"Our manager, Markus, moved the dance with the doubles to the beginning of the show at the last minute. He wanted to start with a modern dance version to create a splash."

She unlocked her hotel room with the room key and moved to let him inside.

"Tell me what brought you to this city besides the studio lights. Do you gamble?"

Rory sighed.

"I gamble until I lose three hundred dollars. Then I stop and look for food. The casinos have excellent restaurants, and smaller restaurants have fun food. I received your two texts."

She was needing food. She blushed.

"Would you like to join the dancers for dinner? They always make room for friendly guests."

"No, actually, I hoped we could eat alone and try fun fast food. I wanted to see you and talk.

Gloria handed him a drink from the mini-bar, and she sat down in one of the comfortable hotel chairs. He kept standing.

"My girlfriend and I were having problems before I did your video and photos. She said that I wasn't paying enough attention to her which is true. Then she said that I was brooding over someone else. She guessed that I was thinking about a dancer, specifically a blue dancer."

She looked guilty.

"We shouldn't have talked at the restaurant after my acceptance by the troupe. The glass of dessert wine from the chef relaxed us more. We delved into areas that we have in common. I did enjoy the conversation, and the chef did select a good vintage wine."

"No, I'm glad we talked. Some feelings were happening when we were close. Seeing you three times wasn't quite enough. I needed to visit with you again. I could have called. However, talking with someone in the flesh is much better when the subject is serious."

Gloria sipped her drink slowly. "How serious?"

His eyes sparkled, "Very serious."

She swallowed.

"My whole focus has been dancing. I'm not sure I want to welcome complications. You present a complication. I'm on tour, and you are far away."

"Ah, yes, think of me as a distraction rather than a complication."

"I might want a distraction with a successful photographer, but still, there's the other thing."

"Distance. Miles apart might be a problem. Is that the only other reason?"

She put her drink down and walked over to him. He pulled her into his arms and kissed her slowly.

Gloria knew she was walking in the dark. His kisses tasted good.

"This seriousness could lead to an affair. An affair might not be what you or I need."

Memories of once being in love were not exactly the best thing that ever happened to her. There

71

were trust issues. Then she remembered how Rory protected her by suggesting she select a different song and dance. She pulled away. Rory gently pulled her back. He wasn't going to let her go so easily.

"How do you know unless we start? There's an old saying; *no time like the present*. I'm willing to take the plunge. At any time, you can say stop, and we will stop."

She kissed him back knowing their future awaited. A lifetime could belong to them. He smelled her sweet lilacs perfume.

"Let's go for a walk on the beach and grab some corn dogs. I need at least two," mentioned Rory.

"You like corn dogs. My dad has a special hotdog night at his place called Gloria's Bistro. His customers flock to the place. Who knew you men were the same type of carnivores?"

They found a small beachside table and ate their corn dogs and French fries. Rory smeared the fries with ketchup, and both fought over the mustard packets.

He dumped pickle relish on her half-eaten corn dog. Gloria looked at the dog. Smiling she held up her corn dog, and he took a bite. She smeared relish on his dog with her finger and held up the corn dog.

He gave her a bite which she ate fast. He laughed and quickly finished the rest. Rory grabbed her hand and licked her finger tasting more relish. Gloria's hand tingled. She bit her lip in delight.

They finished their food watching the ocean water. He tossed their cardboard trays in the garbage.

The air was warm, and the night carried a soft glow from the hotels and casinos. They walked the beach and held hands. Their fingers were interlaced together.

The two young people talked about themselves and their dreams. Gloria wanted to dance in ballet on a huge stage and eventually, teach dancing in her studio. He wanted to keep shooting photographs and expand his photography business.

When they went back to Gloria's room, she invited him to stay overnight. Rory was glad he didn't purchase a hotel room earlier.

He helped her undress and carried her to bed. Rory touched her soft skin.

"I'm not going to stop. I'm here."

Gloria didn't want him to stop.

"Did you need the lights?"

"Only some of the lights," mentioned Rory.

He enjoyed the sparkle of light and laughter in her eyes. They were two people connecting on a strange night. Neither one wanted to be alone. The stars were bright, and the evening air was heavenly.

Two people connected.

In the morning she heard Rory whisper in her ear some special words. They were either Spanish or Italian.

Gloria smiled, "I love you?"

"I'm falling hard for a blue dancer with long legs. Your skin is amazingly soft, your nose is perky, and I like your hair. Do I need to continue? I haven't talked about the best parts. Sweet relish never tasted so good."

"We had fun last evening."

He kissed her and watched her eyes which turned into liquid smoke. He touched her brow.

"I've looked at your schedule, and we can't meet again until Miami."

"You think you can wait that long to see me?" She moved closer, so their bodies touched.

His finger traveled to her cheek and mouth. She kissed his fingers.

"Not fair."

She pouted sweetly.

"All right. I'll move my schedule and will see you on Friday evening in Raleigh. But Charleston is out, I have a meeting with my lawyer and camera operators. They want to become my partners. With the added cash flow, we can hire a manager. That way I will have more freedom to visit you in the cities while you complete your tour."

Gloria was pleased. She glanced at the small clock on the nightstand.

"Oh, my gosh! The bus leaves in fifteen minutes."

They jumped out of bed and threw their clothes on. She stuffed her makeup, jacket, and computer in her small bag. Clothes were sloppily put in the larger bag. Rory grabbed her two bags, and they ran to the elevator and the awaiting bus.

The bus driver was closing the luggage compartments. Rory handed him the large bag. Gloria took her small bag. She dropped it when Rory kissed her lovingly.

All the dancers on the bus saw the two lovers and whistled. Gloria snatched her small bag and took her seat on the bus. Rory ran back to the room to pack and drive home. He would grab breakfast later.

Gloria sat down next to Geri. There was only one seat left on the bus. Geri waited until she stored her bag.

"Our whole troupe saw Mr. Randall. The man didn't have any shirt on nor a belt. He also was barefoot which probably isn't too unusual when a person comes to the beach."

Gloria looked out the window. "Oh, shut up. I didn't notice."

"Get out!"

Gloria looked at her friend and smiled. She sunk lower in the soft seat and almost went to sleep.

"We get that the photographer man is divine."

Gloria wasn't about to explain.

Geri looked at her happy friend.

"Really? No comment. He must have been impressive."

"There are some things that are personal."

"Of course."

Geri wouldn't tell her about her feelings for Dillon until Miami. The two of them might connect now that Gloria was out of the picture.

Anyway, Geri hoped he would.

"Men are so fickle."

Gloria murmured, "We fought over the mustard packet, not the relish. The relish sealed the overnight deal."

Geri grinned. Her friend threw her a bone.

"Have your dad send me jars of his sweet relish for the rest of the tour."

13 Pranks

Rory and Gloria joined the dancers for Friday evening's all-you-can-eat fish dinner, and on Saturday evening they disappeared to their room.

The other dancers were bored. There was no casino at this hotel. They were stuck someplace called Research Triangle Park in Raleigh, North Carolina.

Dillon said, "The closest restaurant has chicken and ribs for takeout. There's a hardware store nearby. The car rental place is fifteen miles away. We would need to take a taxi to get the car."

Dan groaned. "Maybe we can have a mini chess tournament."

"Maybe we should build something and leave it on the balcony, so people know the dancers have been here," suggested Dillon.

Bella stopped reading her magazine. They were in Dillon's room.

"I always liked the horse in a chess game. The horse reminds me of the days of knighthood. The men were gone days, weeks, and months at a time."

Dillon looked at Bella strangely. Clark was staring out the window. Bella smiled innocently.

"That's it. We have two teams and build two trojan horses. When we leave, we put one on my balcony and one on Dan's balcony."

They ordered takeout food from the chicken and rib place which did have delivery to the hotel. The men dancers took a taxi to the hardware store. They purchased wallpaper, wallpaper paste, buckets, brushes, chicken wire, paint, glue, batteries, light bulbs, cords, and electrical items. At the last minute, they included plastic drop cloths to save the carpet. Large cardboard letters were purchased with a small rope.

Saturday night and early Sunday morning, they secretly built the six-foot horses and rigged lights in the horses' eyes. The letters were put together which spelled out, *the dancers were here.*

Sunday evening, they put the horses and sign on the balconies on the tenth floor. They left on the bus early Monday morning to go to their next city.

After the dancers left, the two housekeepers opened the long curtains on the balcony doors and fled screaming from the room. One was yelling something,

"Those freaking Greeks weren't dead after all. Their force was still alive and on the tenth floor."

The hotel called the manager of the Columbia Dance Troupe. Markus Lang apologized to the hotel and would give them free tickets for the two housekeepers and their entire security team.

The security team put the horses in the basement for their annual Christmas party. This was before the news media van took a picture from the hotel across the street and published the article on the news and in the newspaper.

Whenever there was no casino for the dancers, they rigged something on two balconies.

One time they bought mannequins in swimsuits, a large cloth tarp, and painted, *the dancers were here* on the fabric. The mannequins were positioned in different poses with their legs hanging over the railing.

The best one was the Christmas tree they made from chicken bones, rib bones, and crab shells. The tree lights were all blue. They also purchased deer antlers from a local farmer and empty seed bags. The ping pong balls came from a distributor staying at their hotel.

Only one balcony was used for the twelve-foot tree. When the security people picked up the tree, the ping pong balls fell out on the fourth story. The balls bounced back up two stories hitting other balconies before their journey south into the street of grade school children on a walk to the art museum.

The dancers didn't leave Rory and Gloria out of their shenanigans.

A large hanging skeleton was hung over their hotel room doorway. The dancers let Gloria in on the deal. Rory almost had a heart attack when he opened the door. Gloria fell into fits of laughter.

Rory got even and hung the skeleton in the shower to scare her. While Rory was out getting their breakfast, she cut the hands off the skeleton and put them in his briefcase.

When Rory arrived at the airport, he opened the case to get his tickets. He went to the men's restroom and threw them in the trash. Another housekeeper went screaming for security.

To get even, when Rory got back to his studio in New York City, he bought six skeletons to represent the six crazy double dancers. He arranged them in a sitting thinker position with a scary background, took a photo, and sent them each a text. The picture was posted to a social media site and went viral.

Not to be outdone, Dillon hired some of his friends from the local ballet company in New York City to purchase blue-colored shredded paper. They drove to Rory's studio and dumped the paper on top of his sports car. They left a sign, *guess who was here—dancers.*

Rory knew he needed reinforcements. He enlisted Guy and Stan's help. Guy contacted a circus man who owned an elephant. They rigged a large tutu on the elephant. Sitting the elephant next to Dillon's jeep at his mother's place the sign read, *next first-string partner*. The camera operators took a snapshot. The photograph was handed over to the newspaper.

The newspaper friend authored a story about the troupe dancers and mentioned the photograph was payback. Rory sent Dillon a copy of the newspaper to the hotel in the next dance city.

The pranks plus the news media hype was good for business and their manager. Markus left the dancers to their mischievous creativity until they bought a net and tied fifty helium balloons to the cording. The net was placed on the balcony. The net came loose with their sign, *the dancers were here,* and the sign was hanging vertically.

The balloons caught on the hotel tower, and the fire department was called to get the objects down. The fire department bill was sent to Markus who promptly handed the bill to Dillon. The other dancers chipped in to help pay the amount.

Markus was glad the last two shows of this tour were within walking distance of a casino. He would need to get his lawyers to write new contracts for the dance players for next year to include the words, *no pranks or signs allowed in any of the hotels.*

A movie executive was watching the increased media coverage regarding the dancers from the Columbia Dancing Troupe. He looked again at a script that was sitting on his desk. The story was a good one.

His secretary brought the newspaper story to him about the shredded paper incident and sports car. She left to get coffee. He read the article, and there was something there that piqued his interest.

The executive searched his computer and found the Strand business website. Now he was very intrigued. He pushed the button for his secretary.

"Find out information regarding the dancer named Gloria Strand. Get Mr. Silverman on the line."

"Yes, sir, Mr. Chadsworth."

She closed the door etched with the company name of Chadsworth and Silverman Movie Productions.

14 Movie Firm

For the rest of the tour, both Dillon and Gloria held their places within the first string. They also were in the double dancer group in the first performance.

The local ballet company in New York City liked the furor over Dillon that they read and saw in the media. Both dancers updated their resumes.

Rory proposed to Gloria in Philadelphia which was the next to the last city on the tour schedule. They became embroiled in a heated discussion. Gloria wanted to wait a year until they married. She wasn't ready, but she loved him.

Resigning himself to wait a year, he tried to get her to move in with him. She didn't want to upset her old man nor all his patrons. Her reputation would be ruined. Gloria did agree to spend weekends at his place. They came to a truce about their wedding date.

The last city for the dancers was in New York City. Gloria purchased a raft of tickets for her father and their friends for the dance performance. Rory did the same for his friends.

A party was arranged at her father's bistro afterward. Gloria purchased an additional neon sign with the numbers 1,2,3,4 to go alongside Gloria's Bistro and the neon dancer. Before the new sign came, the bistro word lights gave up the ghost. They were broken due to age.

Gloria's father looked at the old sign.

"I never liked the word bistro. The word was your mother's choice."

He threw the bistro part in the dumpster and came back into his place. Her father changed the legal name. The place would be more glamorous. Fresh flowers were ordered. New white cloth tablecloths were ordered and napkins. New lights were placed in the drinks, pop, and coffee area.

Rory drove with Gloria back to New York City in a rental car. The dancers had a week and a half off before the final show. The next day, she visited her father.

Gloria noticed a limousine pull up in their parking spaces in front of her father's place. An elderly white-haired man dressed in a suit and his secretary stepped out of the car. Their chauffeur would wait until their business was done in the *reserved for important people* parking sign.

Gloria looked at her clothes. She wore black tights and a white crop top. Stan was working on the ice machine in the back. She yelled at him that they had especially important customers.

The man approached her.

"You must be Gloria Strand. You look exactly as I imagined. My name is Mr. Charles Chadsworth."

Gloria knew who he was from a picture in a movie magazine. She extended her hand. He shook it.

"Welcome to Gloria's. We're waiting for a new sign. The name will be Gloria's 1,2,3,4. Can I get you a drink or coffee?"

"Coffee with cream. Hot tea if you have the black stuff for my assistant. I did like the neon-shaped dancer figure."

Stan came into the front and washed his hands at a small sink. He saw the pricey limo outside. No one ever parked a limo that nice before at Gloria's place.

He took the coffee pot away from Gloria's shaking hands. He poured the coffee with cream and hot tea. Gloria gave him the cup with the fresh lemon slice and a sugar packet. He grabbed the tiny cup just in case the item was required. He put the items on one of their new copper and silver trays.

Stan deposited the new stoneware cups at one of the tables. The paper cups weren't used anymore unless someone wanted takeout. He was glad the new tablecloths were already on the tables. The place looked classy.

"Is there anything else we can get you?" asked Gloria. "We have some scones from our breakfast menu."

"Sit down young lady. You are the reason for our visit."

Stan flipped the sign on the front door to closed and went into the back room. He called Gloria's father. Guy didn't answer. He was buying candles in fancy glass containers.

Stan came back out by the countertop and cleaned the stool tops. He hung close to Gloria in case she needed him. Then he got a clean rag and polished the wood counter. Stan tried to listen to the conversation.

"I have a script here that seems to be written for a blue dancer like you. If you are interested in a five-million-dollar contract, please sign your acceptance that you have received a copy of the script and won't divulge its contents."

The secretary handed her the paper and a brown packet. Gloria was speechless.

Mr. Chadsworth talked about his company. They liked to find unknown stars. He saw her perform in Atlanta and liked what he saw. He professed to have checked out Rory Randall's business when he saw the newspaper article about the shredded paper incident and the elephant. He liked the man's choice of a sports car.

"Let's get back to the movie. Your dancing skills are perfect for this story. Take three weeks to read the book. A film is usually different from a book, but we will try to hold to the story. We begin filming two months after your New York show with the dance troupe. We will film most of the storyline here in New York City. Oh, there is a male performer in the story, and I can't tell you about the male performer because we haven't contracted with him yet."

"Thank you, Mr. Chadsworth. I am extremely interested. I don't have much acting experience, just college plays. My dancing is top-notch."

"We know your education and dancing background. My company has done some research."

"Then you know there is another dancer. His name is Dillon Andrews."

Mr. Chadsworth laughed.

"Yes, we have heard of Mr. Dillon Andrews. Thank you for mentioning him. We hope you will sign on with Chadsworth and Silverman Movie Productions.

You will have time for your lawyer to review any final terms in the permanent movie contract. I have another appointment and must leave. Our business is done until we hear from you. Here is my card which will ring to my assistant."

Mr. Chadsworth stood as did his secretary. Emily read the two pages and signed the documents. The secretary gave her a copy and put the other one in a briefcase. Her copy, the business card, and the movie script were on the table. Stan held the front door open for them.

Gloria was standing very still. She looked at Stan who locked the door.

"Gloria Strand, the movie star? This is big!"

"You overheard Mr. Chadsworth's conversation?"

"I did."

She leaped in Stan's strong arms, and he swung her around. Her father walked into the back of the bistro and put his fancy candle purchases down.

Stan put Gloria on top of the wood counter. He handed her the packet. He turned on the music. She danced exotically and freely on the top.

Guy watched his daughter in confusion. He knew something happened while he was gone. Guy knew whatever happened must belong to Gloria's dancing dream.

Stan handed Guy the copy of the document his daughter just signed. Guy went to the nearest table, sat down, and read the letter three times.

Gloria stopped dancing and slid off the wood surface with Stan's help. She ran to her father, and he hugged her.

"We're going to be in the movies."

"I think there's a good shot. However, you and Stan must keep quiet until I'm certain."

"Will you tell Rory Randall?"

Gloria thought about her boyfriend.

"I'll try not to tell. He will guess."

"Yes, he will. It's the gleam in your eyes, and the pretty nose in the air that will give you away," said her father.

Gloria couldn't help but disappear to her old room to begin reading the story. She had six hours before meeting Rory. Stan got a tray of salad and milk. He carried the tray to her room.

The sign was flipped to open, and the door was unlocked.

Guy and Stan were whistling a tune. It was Gloria's favorite song. A few patrons walked in and were surprised by the candles on the tables. The place was looking up.

Her father and Stan would hire a server for a day, so they could buy new suits, shirts, ties, and shoes.

Gloria told no one, not even Geri or Dillon.

15 New York & Party

Their performance in New York City was an easy one for the dancers from the Columbia Dancing Troupe. They were used to the routine and moved smoothly through their final number. The dancers graciously bowed, and their manager came out. He also bowed to the audience and the performers. The curtain closed.

Quickly changing out of their costumes, the dancers handed their outfits over to the company. They were allowed to keep the blue jacket.

The only people that could make her party from the troupe were Geri and Dillon. Gloria knew Dan left to go traveling with his male friend, Johnny. The others went home to their families and friends.

At the party, Gloria told everyone about her movie deal. She told Rory the evening before. Dillon also announced that he had been cast by the same movie company in the film. He wasn't the lead dancer in the story but would make six hundred thousand dollars for a few dance scenes.

Geri let them know that she signed on for a second tour with the Columbia Dancing Troupe. Dillon and Gloria didn't tell her they were approached also and declined.

The party was filled with food, laughter, drinks, and music. The catering company cooked on the front sidewalk and made hot sandwiches hoagie style. There was chicken and sliced beef or tacos with freshly shredded vegetables. Cold fruit on long sticks added a nice touch with drizzled white chocolate.

Finally, the food was depleted, and the place was emptying fast. The patrons congratulated Gloria and her father as they left.

The catering company cleared the dishes, garbage, and equipment. The catering chef brought Gloria a foam tray of the wrapped tacos to have the next day. He apologized all the buns and meat were gone due to the carnivore-like neighborhood. She laughed. Gloria didn't mind the veggies.

Dillon went to the restroom. Stan and Rory were helping clear some of the trash. Geri talked with Gloria in private.

"I was blown away by your news regarding the movie deal. I'm glad you will have your shot at stardom. At first, I was jealous, but you are a better dancer. You earned the right to be chosen."

"Thanks, Geri. What are you going to do with a month off from the dance troupe?"

Geri watched Dillon return and talk with the two men at the bar. Gloria's dad was out front laughing with the local police officers.

"My parents have a storage unit that I never knew about. The company called and wanted payment, or else the contents will be placed in the dumpster. I'm going to hire a mover to bring the stuff to my parent's garage. I'll sort and dispose of the items. If I don't get through the junk, the rest can wait for another year."

"It's strange your parents didn't tell you about what was in this storage facility."

Geri volunteered, "I drove to the place, and the owners let me look. My mom has the year written on the outside of the boxes. I imagine there is stuff from when we were in high school together. If there's anything fun inside, I'll save you the items."

Gloria shook her head. She didn't like high school years that much.

"Don't save anything for me. I dated your brother in high school, and we all know how that turned out."

Geri did remember and frowned, "Maybe I should just dump the stuff and not look. I'll think about doing the destruction if the first ten boxes are weird stuff. I need to leave. Dillon is ready. Goodnight!"

The three dancers walked to the back door.

"Geri, I'm glad the troupe asked you to dance again. You did something very right and should be proud."

The two women hugged before Geri and Dillon left. Rory joined Gloria.

"Nice party. Hungry neighborhood."

"I'll share some veggie tacos with you."

Rory shook his head, "No, thanks. I do like these mints your dad keeps behind the bar."

16 Murder in a Garage

The movie was completed. Gloria and Rory went to the movie's opening night as did Dillon with an actor.

Gloria's father was in the hospital with a minor case of pneumonia. Stan stayed behind to be with him. Geri was doing a show with the dance troupe and couldn't be there. Dan was busy elsewhere.

Rory and Gloria went to his apartment for the weekend.

"Now, can we please talk about our wedding?"

Gloria knew she was ready. Rory's patience was wearing thin.

"Yes, but first I need to decompress from this movie deal. I'm tired but not too tired."

Rory kissed her and guided her into his bedroom. He had a designer redo the room while Gloria was filming.

She looked around and saw beautiful white covers against black furniture. The look was modern and refreshing. On the walls were large photographs of her dancing at his studio. There were a few pictures of Rory taking the photographs.

"I love this new look."

Rory released her, so she could snoop in the new bathroom with the white marble walls.

She came back out to him in her soft and sexy black dress. He slowly unzipped and kissed her shoulders. She kissed him back, savoring his sweet mint breath.

After they made love, he held her as if she were the only treasured piece of art in the room. In the morning he woke her with a whisper. She recognized the words. He went to the redesigned kitchen and made her waffles with scrambled eggs.

"What, no meat?"

He laughed.

"I'm trying your vegetarian meals."

"Now that we have chosen a date, what would you like to do today?"

Gloria worried about her future.

"I should probably update my resume. I was thinking of applying to the ballet company. Dillon is going to apply and told me that I should do the same."

"Why don't you hold off on your resume and see how the film does in the ratings? I could use your help in my studio. You have a trained eye that might be useful. Or we can fly somewhere for a two-week vacation?"

"Hmm, a vacation sounds nice. I've always wanted to snorkel."

"Done. I'll call my agent today."

The two of them went on a snorkeling vacation in Greece for two weeks.

When they returned, Dillon called Gloria. She was alone at Rory's apartment.

"Sit down. I have some disturbing news. The police arrested me, and they had to let me go. I was on an airplane, so they couldn't charge me. Thank goodness I went to visit a friend in The Hampton's."

Gloria didn't understand. "Charge you for what?"

Dillon paused. The news was personal, and he was worried about her reaction. "You're at Rory's apartment. I'll be right over."

Gloria made a pot of coffee and let Dillon into the kitchen. She poured them a cup of coffee.

"Geri came home for the long weekend break from her tour. The police have found Geri in her parent's garage. She was stabbed yesterday by an assailant. They couldn't revive her."

Gloria gasped.

"Stabbed by whom? How can she be dead?"

She spilled her coffee and Dillon grabbed a paper napkin.

"Oh, no, poor Geri. I'll never see her again."

He took Gloria in his arms as she cried about the loss. He found a tissue, and she blew her nose. He poured more coffee.

"Do they have any suspects?"

"Not that I'm aware of. She was going through some boxes in her garage. The door was open, so the killer just walked into her space. None of the neighbors saw anything."

"Why would the police suspect you?"

Dillon shook his head.

"I don't know. Geri might have talked to her parents about me. She wanted us to date seriously. With her schedule and my job hunting, there didn't seem a reason. Besides, we were just friends. I liked being friends. The police mistakenly assumed we might have been lovers and quarreled."

"Geri could be irrational when she didn't get her way. Also, she made stuff up when she talked to her parents. Did you quarrel?"

"No, I only called her twice because she called me. We talked over the phone. That was all. She talked about going through boxes. I wasn't paying too much attention."

Gloria frowned.

"You don't think it was someone on the new tour with her?"

"Your guess is as good as mine. I don't know the new dancers. We were a good group and didn't want to kill each other."

"Maybe there was something in the boxes."

Now Dillon's face wrinkled.

"Your idea is a leap. The boxes were old high school stuff per Geri. You went to high school with her."

"Exactly. She was fine until she started on the boxes. Maybe it was someone from her past."

Dillon handed Gloria another tissue. He tried to console her.

"She loved you. Geri told me once that you were the best friend she ever had."

Gloria blew her nose. The crying subsided. She was thoughtful.

"We had our difficulties, but we were good for each other in the end. We both needed to dance. She helped me and vice versa. I can't believe she is gone. I wonder if Jordan will let me have her ballet shoes to hang in my father's place. She would like that."

"I'll ask him for you. I don't want you near him. Geri told me about the car accident."

Rory walked into the kitchen and saw the two dancers. His wife looked bleakly at him.

He spoke quietly.

"I heard on the radio. I'm so sorry sweetheart. Come here."

Gloria went into his waiting arms, and Rory held her close.

Dillon knew it was time for him to exit. They would see each other again at Geri's funeral.

Her brother, Jordan, was in town per the police. Dillon decided not to tell Gloria. She would know soon enough.

17 Geri's Funeral

Guy Strand invited close friends of Gloria's for a wake party at his place. He hired the Italian restaurant caterers to bring Geri's favorite dish of lasagna, garlic bread, and salad. He told the caterers to bring extra olives and tiny, sweet pickles, too.

Her favorite drink was champagne. Stan bought cases of the stuff. He would be one of the servers. They used paper plates, plastic dinnerware, and plastic glasses. No one would notice.

The funeral was large and impressive. The entire ballet troupe and the manager attended the funeral. There were executives from the dancing company. Gloria saw several other limousines pull into the cemetery. She was surprised to see Mr. Chadsworth and Mr. Silverman arrive. Both men approached her group. Dillon, Bella, and Dan stepped aside.

Mr. Chadsworth held out his hand to her father, and the men introduced themselves.

"I was in Atlanta and saw the dancing troupe. I remember Gloria Strand and Geri Sullivan. This is such a tragedy to the dance world. My condolences to the dancers and their families. The large photograph of Geri and her royal blue logo jacket draped over an empty chair made me want to cry. She was so young."

Guy invited the two movie moguls to his bistro after the funeral and the Columbia Dancing Troupe executives. Gloria was surprised a second time that day regarding her father's reaction.

The media vans arrived and took pictures of the dance celebrities. They tried to talk to Gloria, but Rory and Stan wouldn't let them get close.

After the church ceremony, the cars went to the cemetery. Gloria stayed far back from the casket and away from Jordan. Gloria's parents needed help standing. When she saw Jordan leave to talk with the minister, Gloria went to talk with them and extended her condolences. Geri's mother looked frail and incredibly sad.

Dillon did get Geri's dancing shoes. They were her shoes from the Columbia Dancing Troupe. She put them inside a glass frame with a signed picture of her from the dance troupe. A neon star was placed over the box. There was a huge wreath of flowers to match the one sent to the funeral home. A massive sign was spread on the roof of the place with large balloons, *the dancers were here.*

Chadsworth and Silverman admired the shoes and the other artifacts and photographs around the bistro. They were particularly pleased with a recently added picture of little Gloria in her tights and tutu. They met with the Columbia executives and were impressed by their amount of knowledge and the dance films they each liked. Many of the dancers were invited and two-thirds of them showed at the bistro party.

The other room contained champagne, drinks, and canapes. There were old movies of Geri and Gloria dancing together on the wood countertop. Gloria would start each dance with a microphone singing, "1,2,3,4."

She would throw the microphone to Stan after he started the music.

The two young girls danced in a perfectly controlled motion. Their synchronization was unmatched by other dancers their age. The first professional tape together was at age sixteen. The dance showed their expertise. They crossed in front of each other fighting for the spotlight. There were no missed beats.

They included Geri's two tapes for her first application to the dance troupe. Geri's father let Gloria have access to the film. Gloria had difficulty watching one of the videos. The song and ending were her routines. Stan noticed and gave her an okay sign with his fingers. She responded with the same sign.

There were still shots of both girls together that flashed on the large newly installed sixty-five-inch screen television in their extra room.

The Strand family and friends made the newcomers feel like they were part of their normal group. The movie company men watched the homemade movies while having a fun time. They particularly liked the dancing. In the second tape of their younger dances, Geri fell and was caught by Stan, and placed back on the wood countertop. The fall was choreographed into their dance to give the audience a thrill.

Everyone in the room clapped. The popcorn machine added to the noise. The dance music rebounded off the walls when the girls were dancing courtesy of a sound technician hired for the event.

The movie men and their bodyguards even stayed and played a few rounds of poker after their canapes. The neighborhood boys juggled the cars to various parking lots and kept the limousines out front or in their back lot, away from any want-to-be thieves. The bistro was on the fringe of the medium and pour income society.

The funeral and party were befitting of Geri's dance accomplishments and her friendship with the Strands. They counted her as a second daughter and sister.

Geri always wanted to be noticed. The spotlight was always grabbed at the first opportunity. She got her wish and became known as the beautiful young star dancer from New York City. The dance troupe donated an engraved marble stone to her family because Geri helped them with their jumps.

Guy hugged his daughter, Gloria, after the executives left.

"Get out. That's what you need to do after this amazing party that you helped me arrange. Geri would have enjoyed being here."

Gloria nodded.

Rory drove his sports car into the spot the limousine left a few minutes earlier. Gloria was waiting for him. He took her home to the quiet apartment. She needed calm days to get over the loss of her friend. Rory talked to her on the way home. He told her the ballet shoes looked grand.

She started crying. He was glad the dam broke.

"I'm here."

Now she could heal. He escorted her into their apartment where she wouldn't re-surface to the outside world for two weeks.

Finally, Gloria's father came to take her out for lunch and visit Geri's grave in private. She wore dark clothes and glasses. There were no media vans following them. They both needed closure.

People and the police believed Geri Sullivan's death was a random incident. They didn't know her murder wasn't random.

There was a killer who needed to correct things. He knew the best thing to do was get out of town. The more he stayed, the more the police might change their focus.

18 Chadsworth's Proposal

Gloria sat in Mr. Chadsworth's office. She looked out the window at the sunshine. The sky was bluer than yesterday. She brightened as she heard his footsteps. He appeared and held out his hands to her.

"Please sit down. I know it's been only three months since your dear friend died. However, when I saw this script, I remembered how wonderful your family was to me and Mr. Silverman at an incredibly sad time. We agreed that we must at least talk to you."

Gloria swallowed. She wasn't sure she could dance. She hadn't been to the gym or dance studio since Geri's death. She was going to decline any proposal.

Mr. Chadsworth held up his hand.

"I talked to your father. He beat me at poker. I asked how you were doing? He told me you hadn't danced since Geri's death. We are willing to delay filming until you are ready. We were hoping for three months or four. You tell us what you need. First, we want you to read the script."

Gloria calculated in her head. Four months was when she and Rory were to be married. Postponing their wedding would be a problem. She would need to approach her future husband with a different plan. Her depression was lifting, but she knew her body was in a funk. Dancing would bring her out of the terrible mood cycle and get her back in shape.

"Where's the contract? I'll read the script and let you know."

Mr. Chadsworth beamed. The script was made for Gloria. It was a rag to riches story.

"Wonderful, Gloria. You know we loved your home dance movies after the funeral. They were pure, uninhibited fun. The love of dance was evident. That's our theme for this second movie. We want you to sparkle!"

Gloria shook his hand, and he walked her to the elevator.

"We will talk to you soon."

"Yes. Thank you for believing in me."

"You just read the script."

When the elevator closed, Mr. Chadsworth rubbed his hands.

"How I love this job."

He could see dollar signs. The last movie with Gloria was a hit. The next film would also benefit his and Silverman's company.

Mr. Zander deceptively told Chadsworth that Gloria was a particularly good friend, and she volunteered information for his book. Although the book was published by Johnny as fiction, she verified the facts. His comments were a lie.

There was some information in the book about parties Johnny and Dan attended with the other dancers. Those stories were fake. Johnny wasn't invited. He wrote most of his book from screwy ideas in his warped brain. The little research he found online about Gloria was small. He guessed what might have happened after her accident at age eighteen.

Mr. Chadsworth forgot to ask Gloria about many pieces of information inside the book and the glowing words Mr. Zander professed in his office.

19 Movie Talk with Rory

Rory opened the kitchen door and smelled roast beef. He peaked in the oven and saw what looked like homemade pot pies. Gloria heard the buzzer and joined him.

"The pies need ten more minutes. My dad brought them over. The bakery has a daughter who opened a shop next door to them. She makes takeout meat and vegetable pies. We also have a salad."

"Great, they smell delicious. I'll be back after I get into comfortable clothes."

She set the table and made them some hot tea. Rory returned to the kitchen and dinner.

He was three-fourths of the way finished with his pot pie when he noticed she was toying with a piece of beef. Rory finished his meal and pushed away his plate.

"What's wrong, Gloria?"

Rory knew her too well.

"I've started exercising on Monday. I called the gym and dance studio to start tomorrow with my scheduled time slots. There's also a modern dance instructor that teaches a class on Friday that I joined."

Rory was impressed.

"That is wonderful. I'm glad you are getting your mojo back."

"There is something else."

Gloria brought the script from her bedside table and placed the book on the table. Rory picked up the script and read the title and the movie company.

"How much?"

"Eight million dollars and five percent of the box office profits."

He whistled.

"Nice deal. When do they want to start shooting?"

Gloria bit her thumb.

"When I talked with Mr. Chadsworth on Monday, he thought the timeline was three to four months."

Rory stared at Gloria.

"This is Thursday. You've kept this script from me this long plus the exercising?"

"I wanted to read the script first. The exercise was slow. I could barely finish the beginner route. We can get married by a justice of the peace and have a reception party later. You don't want to wait."

Rory put the dishes in the dishwasher and made them more tea. His tea was mint and hers was orange spice.

"Let's go into the living room and talk."

Gloria sat on the soft couch. Rory sat next to her and took her hand.

"The puffy dress, the cathedral, the standing at the altar, the blessing, and the long vows that your father wants are thrown out of the window? You and your family's religious beliefs are important. I don't want to get on the wrong side of Guy. You are his only daughter. He has a lot of clientele who would be upset. No, we'll wait until after the film is complete if you want to sign the contract for the movie."

Gloria kissed him.

"Thank you."

Rory smiled, "I kind of like marrying a richer woman. I could buy a second sports car or a boat."

Gloria wasn't sure where they would park a boat.

"There is one more thing. The author is Dan's friend, Johnny Zander. The book almost mirrors my life. Some parts are plain bullshit. The man was having exotic dreams when he drafted his book. I think you should read the script first, and this strange version of my story. The movie production company has the right to alter the movie. In Zander's book, the lead dancer dies from a car accident. He makes me the lead dancer right before the accident."

Rory felt the alarm bells go off.

"Does Dan know about the book?"

"I called him. He didn't know about Johnny's new book. Dan called me back a day later after swiftly reading the story and apologized profusely. He told me that he only briefly mentioned me in the past. Johnny researched the rest. I told him most of the book was make-believe. Dan has moved out of their apartment and won't have anything more to do with the man."

"Ouch, it looks like we created a problem."

Gloria went to the kitchen to bring back some chocolate cookies. She handed one to Rory. He looked at her. She handed him her cookie.

"Zander created his mess. We didn't have anything to do with his horrible book. I've made an appointment with Mr. Chadsworth to talk about the script. I'm going to decline Zander's story and any movie deal. If there is a book about my life, I will someday author my own story and let Chadsworth, and Silverman have the first crack at the movie. If they have a different script from a different author, then I will be interested in a new contract for a movie."

"What will you do in the meantime?"

Gloria knew the answer.

"I thought I could either send my resume to the local ballet company or hire an author to write my own story."

Rory laughed. "Or you could teach others how to dance. The building next to my studio is up for rent."

"Now that is good news and a nice idea, but a dance studio should come later once my name is well-known."

Rory kissed her.

"People who like ballet do stop you on the streets. You are already famous. Since you're feeling better, I thought we could go to bed early tonight. What do you say?"

"Then you are all right with my decision?"

"Yes. I met Zander once and didn't like the man. I think his writing a book about you stinks. The man has a dark side. He's a user. Dan was correct in dropping him. However, Zander won't be pleased to not receive a movie deal."

"I'll ask Mr. Chadsworth to explain to Johnny Zander that the timing is not right. We have other plans right now. A wedding is more important to us."

Gloria was glad Rory wasn't going to read Zander's book. There were some things in his story that Rory didn't know about her. Zander guessed at some of her story facts. Now was not the time to tell Rory. She promised her father that she would tell him soon. Rory did have a right to know about her history.

Rory saw her hesitation. Gloria leaned into her husband and kissed him passionately. The time was ripe for the two lovers to go to bed. Love, in the beginning, is always better. Gloria didn't want to rock the boat. Unwelcome news could wait.

Rory led the way to their bedroom with more cookies. He gave her one.

20 Dad's Word of Caution

She sat at her father's bistro talking with him about the dropped movie deal. Stan was making the day's first batch of coffee. He was listening to their conversation like he always did.

"I understand your reasons. This Johnny Zander person sounds terrible."

Gloria brought the book, so her father could read what the man wrote and quietly remove the object from her and Rory's apartment. The author's photo was on the back.

"He is creepy looking, and the photographer caught his bad side. I don't think he likes humans. He called us girls the G-strings."

Guy looked outside at the people bustling on their way. Cars zoomed past in the street. He could see the bakery was doing good business today.

"The man is nasty, then."

"Read the book dad, and you will see how bad."

Her dad picked up the book and read the table of contents. He turned to the last chapter and read for a few minutes.

"This book is crap. Zander kills you off?"

"Yes, he does."

"Well, that dirty bastard. If he walks into my place of business, I might have an urge to shake him silly. On second thought, he could sue me. The sidewalk is the city's property. Maybe we can get some stale bread from the bakery."

Stan joined them. "What do we do with the bread?"

Gloria informed Stan that he didn't want to get stuffed.

Stan understood and seconded the choking thought.

"Zander also talks about my accident with Jordan. He made stuff up."

Her father went to the refrigerator and came back with two deviled egg sandwiches. He handed one to Gloria. She ate this type of cold sandwich for breakfast since she was little. This one also contained a ham slice.

"I put the ham slice inside. You need protein if you are into dancing again."

She took a bite as did her father.

"In the meantime, I'm glad you have started. You seem happier already after two weeks of exercise. Ms. Jones from the bakery gave me the name of your modern dance instructor. How do you like him? One of her patrons raved about the man."

"I've had three lessons with Jake Forsyth. The lessons are going well."

Her father sighed.

"Has Rory met Mr. Forsyth yet?"

"No, why would he?"

Her father and Stan looked at Gloria.

"Why is it that you men immediately think that a single man wants a woman?"

Stan interjected, "A man will always want a beautiful, sexy-looking woman, especially one in tight-fitting leotards and a skimpy top."

Gloria looked at her outfit and crop top. Tomorrow she was going to wear baggy pants and a top that covered everything. She might sweat a little more but sweat could be a deterrent.

"I'll make a point to introduce Mr. Forsyth to Rory."

Both men looked alarmed.

"What? Isn't that what you wanted me to do?"

Both men shook their heads.

"I get it. I should not introduce Rory because the man is freaking gorgeous, has a great body, and comes from a rich family. Rory doesn't like male dancers. Plus, Mr. Forsyth dances with women in a private studio which is different from the rules that exist for a professional ballet company."

"Now you are on the right track," offered Guy.

Gloria went home to find Rory in their apartment. She put her gym bag away in their closet. She peeked inside the freezer. There were some frozen meals left for dinner and a frozen butterscotch pie.

"Rory, you're home early. I stopped and talked with my father about the defunct movie deal."

"Good. I went by the newsstand on my way home. They carry the latest magazines. Here's a dance magazine and guess who made the cover? The article says he owns Diamond Dancing Studio which is where you are taking a class. Tell me he is not your instructor?"

Gloria saw a picture of Jake in a tuxedo with one of his students going to a ballet. Rory looked at her. She knew he was not happy.

"Look, I dance with jocks in tights all the time. They don't have the impact they used to have. Geri and I would get excited when we were teenagers. I've grown out of the phase of awestruck. Besides, I'm with you now. You're a more handsome jock."

"He's filthy rich and likes female dancers."

Gloria shouldn't have used the word jock twice. She was glad the article showed the man in a tuxedo. In tights, there existed an awesome body. Gloria wasn't sure about the brain part. She thought about the Adonis statue in white Carrara marble which was a study of the male torso. The body was perfectly proportioned. She wondered if Adonis had a brain.

"I only have two lessons left. I won't sign for the next set."

Rory saw a brief flash of the dreamy look in her eyes.

"Make that one lesson left. The one where you tell him you have made other plans."

Gloria was speechless. Her soon-to-be-husband was jealous. Being engaged didn't exactly give a man an immediate secure feeling. He got off the kitchen stool and left the room. He came back.

"I didn't hear an answer."

His eyes looked stormy.

"You know Jake Forsyth?"

"Yes."

Gloria heard the anger in his voice. There was a story regarding Jake. Now was not the time to ask her fiancé.

"I'll drop his class."

"Thank you," said Rory. He went to their exercise room. She could hear him select the hard bicycle route.

Gloria threw the magazine in the trash and watered her herb plants.

Dillon called her. Gloria stepped outside to their patio. She sat on the lounge chair.

"I have a dancer who is looking to take some modern classes. I called the Diamond Dancing Studio, and they gave me your name as a reference."

"Bad timing, I'm afraid. I'm going to be dropping Jake's class," said Gloria.

"His class was that bad?"

"No, I have a husband who has a problem with the man."

There was a long pause on the other end.

"I'll tell my friend she should check out some other studios."

"Good decision." Gloria hung up and went inside.

Eventually, Rory came out to the living room with a towel wrapped around his head. He sat on the ottoman directly in front of her.

"My ex-girlfriend dated Jake before she met me. After we broke up, she went back to him for a couple of months just to irritate me. I don't want Mr. Forsyth to have any part of us. Also, the thought of him touching you made me mad. There, I don't want to talk about the man anymore."

Gloria nodded. She understood. Rory went to finish taking a shower. She texted her father to inform him that she was dropping the Forsyth class.

Rory came out from his shower and sat next to her. He kissed her. She kissed him back.

Gloria worried about the future. There were many items left on her list to complete.

"We'll be fine," said Rory. "Tomorrow is our appointment with the church people. I have some songs in mind. Your father sent me a memo of his twenty favorite songs."

Gloria looked at the ceiling.

"Oh, no, he likes very old songs."

"Exactly. I could only find one that was upbeat from his list."

Gloria knew which songs were Guy's favorites.

"We can squeeze three or four of the songs in the front part of the ceremony while people are being seated. That should make him happy. I'll select those songs for us. Show me your other ones."

The two lovers selected the rest of their wedding songs together. They already wrote their vows and chose the outline for their wedding service.

After the church meeting, Rory would drop her off at the dressmaker's shop for her final fittings. Gloria was happy with her large, gathered net dress. There was a second satin dress for the reception. Their flowers were blue iris and white roses because their wedding was in mid-June. The irises should be plentiful.

The bakery produced a small wedding cake replica. They were meeting at the bakery for a tasting. Gloria and Rory would decide which one of the meals they wanted and inform the caterers.

Their wedding plans were moving swiftly to a conclusion. They couldn't find a hall for the venue and decided to use Rory's studio. The parking was better there, the rooms were larger than the bistro, and there was security plus cameras. They would rent RV's for the people to change outfits. Gloria would change in Rory's office.

Rory was excited about marrying Gloria.

21 Wedding List

A dancer from Gloria's dancing troupe was one of her bridesmaids. Bella and Clark Reine were invited to their wedding. Bella and Stan's girlfriend were the bridesmaids.

The bridesmaid gowns were azure blue netting and iris blue satin tops with white bows. Gloria picked up the bridesmaid dresses along with her two wedding gowns. The dresses were taken to Rory's studio and locked away in a newly cleaned closet.

Gloria looked at her list, and the items were all checked off with the date and time. She reviewed Rory's list. He forgot about the tuxedos. Gloria called him.

"Hi, my wonderful, almost wife. I'm looking at my list. The chauffeurs were hired last week, and the hotel rooms are booked. I've sent all the deposits, but I think that I missed an item."

"You forgot the tuxedos."

"Not really, I decided to buy tuxedos. Dillon already owns one in the style that I purchased for my camera operator. His appointment in New York City for the fitting is in two weeks. I'll send him a reminder note. My tuxedo is in my closet at the apartment. My suit is in the black bag. You've seen me wear mine before, and the suit was recently cleaned. My white shirt gets picked up from the cleaners this afternoon."

Gloria heard keys clicking.

"There, now I'm done with my list. You do know I have a key to the closet at the studios."

116

He rattled the key chain.

"Oh, no, you don't. It's bad luck."

"Some old women made up the theory to scare the men from seeing their brides without makeup."

"You've seen me without makeup."

"I have, and I'm not going to let some old bat scare me off."

Gloria couldn't help but laugh.

"I'll wait until our wedding day and surprise you," said Rory.

"Oh, no. No funny stuff. You can tell Dillon to stop thinking about anything weird. No half-naked mannequins, plaster horses with lights, bones, ping pong balls in trees, helium balloons, or signs."

"Dillon asked me about rice."

Gloria screamed, "No!"

She could visualize a ballet dancer made totally of sticky rice dressed in a bikini.

Rory knew not to push Gloria. She was getting testy lately the closer the wedding date came. He could almost feel her becoming unglued.

"Don't worry. I'll talk to Dillon. I promise no funny stuff. Is glitter okay?"

Gloria sighed. She tried to imagine what Dillon could do with glitter.

"No dropping glitter from an airplane."

Rory was taken aback.

"How did you guess?"

Gloria was going to kill Dillon sooner rather than later.

"Tell him I know what type of underwear he wears, and I'm going to remember when it's his big day."

"Gloria, that's pretty low," chuckled Rory.

"Do you want me to send you the red underwear he parked in our room in Atlantic City?"

There was silence on the other end.

"Now I'm going to kill him. I can always ask my partner to be the other groomsman."

Gloria needed to calm Rory down. She shouldn't have mentioned the underwear.

"I received the tickets today for our honeymoon in Shoal Bay, Anguilla, in the Caribbean. The place opened recently and looks marvelous. I can hardly wait to get us away from here and be all alone."

Rory wanted to be very alone with Gloria. Their lives were too busy sometimes with well-meaning relatives and friends.

"We should have gone to the Justice of the Peace. I could be sitting on a beach with you. You're much prettier than a half-naked glitter mannequin."

"And sexy and hot and great in the sack and steaming!"

"You aren't playing fair. I'm doing these stupid accounting papers and getting turned on by my almost-wife."

Gloria was happy they were talking about fun stuff.

"I'll let you go. I'm picking up some Chinese food for supper, so you can come right home."

She crossed off the tuxedos and got ready to go to the bank for travel money and the Chinese takeout place. The wedding was two weeks away.

Before going to the bank, she bought some white lilies and went to Geri's gravesite. The flower shop didn't have the yellow lilies on hand. There already was a fresh bouquet of red roses lying near her stone. Jordan was in town. Gloria heard a car backfire and quickly looked around.

Her heart stopped beating for a moment. There was no one in the cemetery this time of day. She turned back to the stone and left a small charm bracelet of ballet dancers. Geri always wanted to wear her bracelet. Gloria didn't need the good luck charms anymore. She tucked the bracelet under a loose piece of grass and left.

On the way home, Bella called. Her husband, Clark, was going on a fishing trip on the weekend of Gloria and Rory's wedding. Clark would not be in attendance.

Gloria disconnected the call.

"How very odd?"

22 Wedding and Honeymoon

Gloria was dressed in her white full-length gown. The top was white satin with lace and crystal beading. There were gathered layers of the netting fabric. Her hair was pinned up in curls with white rose accents. The tiara glittered with silver gold fire.

She looked at herself in the full-length mirror. There was a knock at the door. She unlocked and peeked through the crack. It was Rory dressed in his black tuxedo. He looked grand and very handsome.

"Let me in."

"No, Rory."

"I told you I would wait until our wedding day. Our day is here. Now I'm ready."

"No."

He passed a long white box through the crack. She looked inside and saw a diamond necklace. They saw the necklace in a store window last week.

"I love the necklace."

"You'll need help with the clasp," encouraged the waiting groom.

She let him inside the room. Rory looked at her and grabbed her. He kissed her lips. She would need to redo her makeup. Gloria saw the love in his eyes. He whispered to her.

"You look like my heavenly ballet dancer. I can hardly wait."

She nodded. She would show him what he was going to receive later. Gloria lifted her dress, and he saw she wore blue nylons and a white satin garter belt.

He tried to touch her.

"No, you don't. The nylons will run. Not until after the pictures."

Rory looked at her. He would wait. They would be flying breathlessly this evening. He wanted the show to be over. But first, there was a formal route to take with family, friends, and other guests. She deserved her moment in the spotlight as a bride. He bowed low.

"The prince will await in a carriage for his beautiful woman."

There was a knock at the door.

"Hurry!"

Quickly, he fastened her necklace and left. Gloria redid her lipstick and touched the necklace. She was more than ready. Her heart was beating excitedly.

Guy knocked and took her outstretched hand. A guard would watch her room.

She stood with him at the back of the cathedral and walked slowly down the white carpeted aisle when the music played. The rows were decorated in white roses. She was amazed the building was almost full.

Gloria saw Rory waiting for her at the altar with four candelabras blazing brightly.

He gave her his arm, and they stood together.

They were solemnly married. The words of the ceremony were special. She liked being called Ms. Randall before they walked down the aisle to the large wooden front door.

She lifted her skirt, and they raced down the steps to the carriage. The horses pulled the open carriage around the park. They waved to the onlookers. Then Rory took his wife in his arms.

"I told you there would be a carriage."

Their limousine was waiting for them after their short ride. Upon arriving at the reception, she changed into the second tighter-fitting white satin dress. Rory helped her out of the blue-colored nylons. He put the white garter in his pocket for later.

The married couple met all kinds of her family and their friends at Randall's studio. The reception was loud and noisy.

The food was shrimp or bite-size steak with lots of small fried potato balls and various sauces. There were eight salads and of course, the cake. They choose a white cake with side bowls of fruits and nuts.

Their wedding day was perfect, and there were many pictures taken by Rory's camera crew. She hugged her father and the rest of her wedding party goodbye. They were staying at a hotel for the night and flying to their honeymoon in the morning.

Upon reaching their room, Rory turned on the lights. There was white satin G-string underwear strung over their bed in a canopy formation. He picked up the card from Dillon.

The dancers were here.

Gloria shook her head. Rory untied two of the G-strings. He motioned for her to come to sit by him on the bed. They put the G-strings around their champagne glasses and sent a text to Dillon.

We're glad you're not here. From Mr. and Ms. Rory Randall.

When they arrived at their room in Anguilla, there was a large bottle of champagne from the dance troupe and white lilac flowers from Gloria's father.

They went slow-dancing at their beach hotel, bathed in the pools, and did a little scuba-diving. Both needed some space from the world to reinforce their strength and to bond their love. Their future looked bright.

However, danger waited for their return.

23 Bella

The newlyweds returned home to their new life. They drove by Guy's place to visit with Gloria's father before going home.

Dillon called Gloria. He tried Rory's number, and then changed his mind. Gloria immediately picked up her call.

"Dillon, we just arrived and are at my father's place. How are you?"

"I'm fine. Put Rory on the phone."

Gloria handed Rory her phone. Rory walked over to the front door and turned the lock. He motioned for Stan to lock the back door. They watched as Rory took a pen and paper out of his pocket. He wrote an address down.

He looked at the three people watching him. Rory sat down.

"There is shocking news. Another dancer was targeted. Bella was murdered this morning after Clark left to go to his dance exercise. She was stabbed by an unknown intruder. The police are worried there might be a serial killer on the loose targeting female dancers from the Columbia Dancing Troupe. They have notified the company, and the company will be notifying the dancers. They sent me a text a few minutes ago. We need to look at a bodyguard for Gloria."

"Oh, my, gosh, she was at our wedding. Clark must be devastated. How can we help?"

"I have the address of the funeral home, the date, and time for her service. All we can do is show our support."

"I can't believe I would be a target. What do I do about a bodyguard when I'm out exercising, dancing, and shopping?"

"I can contact my security company to get names of people they would recommend."

Her father was visibly upset.

"Gloria can come here when the security person isn't available to watch her. Stan and I have guns and are proficient at hitting a target. Gloria also knows how to shoot."

Guy went to a drawer, unlocked the mechanism, and handed over the permit license with the gun to his daughter.

Gloria pocketed the piece in her bag. The gun would be kept at their place. Rory told them he kept guns at the studio and would give Gloria a key.

Stan watched his friends. He remembered the lovely woman from the wedding.

"If the police don't catch this person, we need to do something," mentioned Stan.

Gloria looked at her father who nodded in agreement. Rory felt a pact was made between the three people in the room, and he was the outsider.

"Don't worry, Rory, we will count you into the plan. For now, you attend the funeral. I have some friends in the police department that I can talk to about Bella's murder. There wasn't much from Geri's death, but now there are two murders. The police will be more cooperative."

Guy looked at Stan.

"I'll call the security company, and we'll beef up the bistro tighter than a tick."

Rory said, "I'll notify my team. Gloria, we are ready to go home. You look frazzled."

When they reached the apartment, Rory checked all the locks and the security system. He was busy on his phone with his partners and then their security people.

Gloria went to their bedroom and unpacked. The laundry pile was high. The laundry would have to wait until a bodyguard arrived. The laundry facility was three doors down and not very secure.

"We need to catch the dance killer."

Her happiness from her wedding and honeymoon were dimmed by the recent events. Gloria wondered when her life would be normal again.

"Bella, you didn't deserve this."

24 Charm & Search

The bodyguard arrived at the apartment to escort Gloria Randall to her classes. She drove in the opposite direction and approached an expensive home. The remote control was sitting in the ashtray.

Per Geri Sullivan's dad, they wouldn't be home, and she could look in the boxes in their garage to see if she could find her silver ballet bracelet. She told them a slight fib. Gloria knew the bracelet was at the cemetery.

Her car was parked in the garage. The bodyguard helped her move some of the cardboard boxes. Gloria found the four boxes that she wanted. They were the last four years of high school. The rest of the boxes were not as important.

After two hours, the only thing she found was a missing dancer from her charm bracelet. This dancer was enameled and wore a blue ballet dress. Geri and Gloria loved this charm. They shared the charm. She pocketed the small object.

Suddenly, she heard a car in the driveway. Gloria motioned for the bodyguard to keep quiet. She slid over to the window and looked outside.

Her eyes widened. Jordan was getting out of his car and entering the front door of the house. He was the last person she wanted to see. No one knew she was there except Geri's father. He didn't like Jordan, so she wasn't worried about him telling. She prayed Jordan wouldn't come into the garage.

After ten minutes, he came back out in his tennis clothes and racket. Jordan got in his car and drove away. Gloria felt relieved. The bodyguard pocketed his weapon.

"I must go into her bedroom on the second floor. You stay here in case Jordan comes back. You can sneak out the side door and distract him at the front door by being a salesperson or pool person. Then I can escape. He is someone I do not want to mess with or visit."

The bodyguard was going to object.

"There's no one in the house. It's also the maid's day off. I'll be fine."

Gloria went through the laundry room and kitchen to the stairwell. Her tennis shoes were quiet on the tile floor. The stairwell was in a large foyer. She saw the tiled star in the center of the floor and the large four-foot wrought iron chandelier. She remembered Geri telling her the workers put in special bracing because of the weight.

Touching the wood and wrought iron railing, she hurried to the second floor and found Geri's room. Everything was tidy. Nothing was changed since her death other than cleaning and laundry.

She sat on the bed and looked at the picture book from Geri's bookshelf. Many of the pictures were of the two of them. She thought it odd there were no pictures of Jordan or her with Jordan. Gloria slipped out a few of her favorite pictures from the book. She put the pictures in her pocket.

Looking in the closet, she moved clothes hangers around. She touched Geri's royal blue logo jacket and almost caved. There was nothing in Geri's shoe or purse closet. Feelings of frustration and sadness were hitting her. She looked around the beautiful rich girl's room.

"Talk to me, Geri. If you found an item of importance, where would you hide the object?"

There was a stuffed doll on the bed. The doll was a large ballet dancer girl with a black velvet top and black satin ballet slippers. The tutu was white with a red ribbon around the waist. The ballet dancer looked like Geri.

She picked up the doll, and a small book fell from the long white netting in the skirt. Gloria didn't have a chance to read the book because the doorbell rang.

A worried look appeared in her eyes. She must have been in the closet when Jordan came back to get his head and armbands. Gloria tiptoed to the top of the stairs with the book.

She overheard the bodyguard talking to Jordan at the front door. She ran back to the bedroom and placed the ballet dancer doll on the bed in the same position. Gloria closed the closet door and made a glance around the room. The room looked the same as before.

She crept down the hall and stairs. She waved at the bodyguard to let him know she was exiting the house. Gloria walked silently behind Jordan. She was glad the lilac cologne was not used this morning. Otherwise, Jordan would have turned around.

Going through the laundry room to the backyard, she was pleased that Geri's parents never bought a dog.

Stopping by a large bush near the garage side door, she waited. The bodyguard was walking across the street selling his fake wares and story. Gloria watched in total amazement. She saw the back of Jordan's car as he went out of the driveway. She exhaled.

"That was too close for me. Rory and my dad would kill me if they knew I was here."

The bodyguard joined her, and they went inside the garage. He put the boxes back on the shelves in date order. Gloria was satisfied. The garage door opener was placed on a shelf like she was told to do by Geri's father.

They looked at the street, and there were no cars. She hit the opener, her bodyguard drove out, and she hit the close button barely ducking under the descending garage door.

Halfway down the street, she realized the book must have fallen out of her pants. Gloria let the bodyguard out. She waited. He came back holding the small book.

"You dropped the book near the garage door. We're fine. You can go to dancing class now."

When she reached class, Gloria put the book in her bag with her ballet shoes and zipped the items shut.

The bag was put in a locker, and she rolled the lock numbers on the cheap lock.

She danced an hour longer than usual. The bodyguard waited for her to get her dance bag. Gloria looked in horror at the lock. The lock was open and laying on the floor. The bodyguard walked over.

Gloria saw the zipper was undone. The book was missing.

"Someone from the Sullivan neighborhood watched and followed us. They must have seen me pick up the red book," said the bodyguard in disgust.

"Jordan has the book. He's the only one that saw you beside the neighbor across the street."

"We were outsmarted. These locks are easy to break. The man took his time and talked to the neighbor. He didn't need to follow us. He already knew where you were going. His sister used the same studio."

Gloria frowned. She found the book that Geri hid. Jordan might have been looking for the book also. The handwriting in the book belonged to Jordan. It suddenly dawned on her. Geri read what was inside the book.

"The book was Jordan Sullivan's diary."

The bodyguard knew about the Sullivan girl's murder.

"Possibly the book is incriminating evidence; how interesting? We have found a bad boy. He sneaks around and steals back his beloved diary."

Gloria was thinking the same thing.

"He'll destroy the book."

"If he does get rid of the evidence, you and I are the only ones that will know. You need to tell Rory or your father."

Gloria thought about the idea.

"No, not yet. I'll talk to someone calmer."

They went to the bistro. Stan was coming off his shift. Gloria detained him in the parking lot in the back. She explained what happened. Stan shook his head.

"We can't go to the police. Approaching Jordan is, without question, a bad idea. Promise me, no more excursions to the Sullivan residence."

"You don't think Geri would have copied the book?"

Stan gave her a look.

"All right. I'll let you tell my father when you think he's in a good mood."

"Gee, thanks, Gloria. I'd as soon be cast in plaster stone."

"I'll tell him tomorrow," offered Gloria.

Stan hesitated. Gloria noticed.

"My girlfriend and I went to the courthouse and were married yesterday. Her daughter and my wife will be moving in with me next week."

Gloria hugged Stan. "How wonderful! Congratulations. We'll buy you a great present and send it over this week."

The bodyguard dropped her off at home. He made sure the apartment was secure and saw Rory drive into the parking space below. Rory opened his apartment door.

"How did things go today?"

The bodyguard smiled.

"She danced."

Rory went inside.

Gloria was taking a shower washing away any dirt she touched inside the boxes. It was the fingerprints from Jordan's book. She felt something odd when she touched the book. The hatred seemed to ooze from the ink Jordan used. She looked at a finger. She scrubbed again at the blue ink color.

Gloria stepped out of the shower. She would tell her husband the good news regarding Stan. Her mind was thinking about presents.

When she stepped out of the shower and grabbed her towel, Rory was holding the charm. The piece must have fallen out of her pants pocket. He handed her the piece and smiled.

"I'll make supper tonight. You look good in a towel."

25 Zander's Threat

The next day Gloria went to her father's place. When she arrived, Stan pointed at her father's calendar. She read the doctor's appointment date and time.

"He's gone."

Stan nodded and went to the backroom to bring more coffee grounds and filters. Gloria saw the front door open and was concerned.

"Mr. Zander, is there some reason you are in this neighborhood? I didn't know you were in the city."

The man looked around the place and came over to her. He stuck out his arm with a letter. Gloria took the envelope and saw a lawyer's name on the return address.

"I'm suing you, Chadsworth and Silverman Movie Productions for defamation of character, fraud, and whatever else we can accumulate."

Gloria didn't understand what he was talking about.

"I don't know why you would want to sue me."

Zander looked around the room. "The movie people dropped my book. They accused me of copying your life story. Mr. Chadsworth told me his firm won't do business with me because of what you said about my book. He said they have selected a different author and a different book. I get paid nothing. My lawyer wants me to sue."

Gloria was trying to put logical sense to his words.

"I haven't talked to Mr. Chadsworth in five months. I didn't know they were doing a second movie."

Mr. Zander stepped closer.

"I don't believe you. They are paying you not to dance in my script. You and the movie company have cut me out. I'm wise to your little scheme. You also were able to convince Dan to drop me."

Now Gloria was mad.

"Dan is a nice and very smart person. Unfortunately, you stole my life story and made untrue statements in your book. He decided to leave you. I guess he has had enough of your negativity and shenanigans. Get out!"

Stan put the box of supplies he was carrying down and moved to Gloria's side.

"Mrs. Randall is done talking. The door is behind you. I suggest Mr. Zander that you make your exit right now. If you don't leave, there are many ways to throw or drag you out. I imagine the cement is mighty solid and scratchy."

Zander looked at Stan and his muscles. He didn't want to tangle with the man. He spun on his heels and yanked open the door. Gloria's father blocked his exit.

"Get out of my way old man."

Gloria's father let go of the door, stepped aside, and stuck out his foot. He remembered the photo on the back of the writer's book. He knew this guy was the creep. Zander tripped and fell.

"I'm going to sue you, too, old man."

Guy wished he had a box of stale bread to trip the man or stuff him. Now his leg would be sore. He bent down and spit on the sidewalk. Then he opened the door of his bar, went inside, and gently shut the door.

"Well, I missed a good show this morning. Get me an orange juice and tell me about the creep that fell accidentally on public property. I only own the cement on the other side of the door where my outside tables and chairs are located. The city will be delighted to squash the bugger."

Gloria opened the letter, read the contents, and handed the letter to her father. Stan read the letter over her father's shoulder.

"He wants five hundred thousand dollars from you and is also suing the production company for two million dollars. The man is daft. Won't Mr. Zander be surprised when he gets his first lawyer's bill? I'll call our lawyer for you, or should we use Rory's lawyer."

Gloria took the letter back and placed the envelope in her bag.

"Rory's lawyer is meaner."

"We'll choose him."

Stan motioned to Gloria. She saw her father turn around.

"There's more excitement than the sneaky little Zander-bugger who tripped?" asked Guy.

Gloria winced. She hated telling her father about her sneaking around.

"Yesterday, I went with my bodyguard to Geri's house. I found a small red diary in her doll dress in her bedroom. Her dad said I could check some old boxes from high school days and take any mementos. I took the book and went to the gym with the book in my bag. The bag was in the locker. Someone broke the lock and stole the book. I only saw the handwriting, and the book was a diary."

Guy watched Gloria's expression. He knew who wrote and stole the diary.

"Jordan."

"Yes. The book contained his handwriting."

Her father looked in the distance.

"Does Rory know?"

"No."

Stan brought the glass of orange juice. Guy took a long drink.

"The man was on my list of suspicious subjects. This confirms there is massive evil in him. We don't know the extent. Don't ever be crazy to go to their home again."

"I won't. But how do we get the police to dig further into Geri's murder?"

Her father thought for a few minutes.

"We have to use the police first. I'll make the call."

The police patrol around the Sullivan neighborhood increased. Jordan booked a cruise to get away from his parent's home.

26 Contract & Coffee Shop

Rory picked Gloria's phone off the counter to see who called. He saw the call was from the Chadsworth and Silverman Movie Production firm.

He heard the doorbell ring, and a messenger arrived with a package for Gloria. Rory signed the receipt. He placed the package on the counter.

Making some tea and scrambled eggs, he punched the toaster button. The English muffins were ready. The butter and jelly were put on a tray.

Assembling the rest of the breakfast, he brought the tray into their bedroom. Rory waited until Gloria was done eating. He was enjoying his scrambled egg. There was sausage, onions, and green peppers inside. Gloria's contained cheese and mushrooms.

"A package has arrived for you, and your phone has a voicemail."

Gloria went into the kitchen and looked at the package. She listened to her voicemail.

Rory came into the kitchen with the tray and dirty dishes.

"Aren't you going to open your package?"

"I'm not sure."

Rory took the scissors out of the drawer and made a slit on the top of the package. He took the script out and glanced at the contract.

"Nice deal. This one is better."

Gloria knew the amount.

"Mr. Chadsworth mentioned ten million and ten percent of ticket sales in his phone message."

"What do you think about my signing the contract?" asked Gloria.

Rory put the dishtowel down and sat on the high stool.

"They will have security while you are on the set. We would need to keep our man here and hire another one when they shoot in Vermont. I don't mind traveling with you and staying with you part of the time. We might have fun on weekends exploring the countryside. There are also good restaurants around the water."

Gloria turned the pages of the contract. Rory's lawyer already approved the document. She pulled a pen out of the desk drawer.

"You should read the script first."

"I already have read the script. This is the one with the agreed legal changes."

Rory shook his head.

"I only got the pdf file last night. I immediately sent the contract to your lawyer. You fell asleep, and I went into the exercise room to read."

"Okay, no gym or dancing class today. I want you to rest. I'll work from home."

"If you work from home, I won't get any rest."

Rory's eyes gleamed.

"No, you don't. I'm going shopping while you work. I'll buy you some winter clothes."

She kissed her husband goodbye and waited for her bodyguard named Edwin. He arrived and Gloria went shopping for wool items, new boots, a jacket, and a hat. She went to the men's section and did the same for Rory. Edwin selected some clothes for himself. He purchased a trapper's hat and grabbed the fishing net from the display. Vermont would be cold, and the fishing might be good.

The clerk told Edwin the net wasn't for sale. The bodyguard believed everything in the store carried a price tag. The clerk looked at the pole. There was no tag. Edwin ripped the sales tag off a shirt and pressed the sticker on the pole.

The sales clerk called security.

The security man came, took one look, and slapped Edwin on the back.

"What's the problem, bro? Edwin Sherman, you dirty dog. You are an absolute crazy sight for my handsome eyes. How long has it been since we went fishing together?"

"Too long. Since when did your eyes get handsome? They still look too large and ugly to me. I want to buy the net for a trip to Vermont."

The guard looked at the sticker.

"Boy, ring up the sale."

Edwin asked his guard friend for a cart for their multitude of packages. They used the service elevator to take the bags to their car.

"Catch a gigantic fish for me and send me the photo."

Edwin laughed.

"You just want to keep your bragging rights. Won't you fall over dead when you see the sucker I'm going to catch?"

The two men slapped each other on the back. The security guard left.

Gloria and her bodyguard walked across the street. She told him there was a large fish market where they were filming.

"Na, I don't want to buy a fish."

Now it was Gloria's turn to grin. She showed him a brochure of the fish market men holding a huge salmon. It wasn't the salmon that caught his attention. The fish case behind the men contained a huge octopus.

"Now there's a thought. I wrap the octopus around the salmon and take a selfie."

Gloria thought Dillon Andrews and Edwin Sherman should meet. Their dry sense of humor was the same.

They entered the busy coffee shop. He found Gloria a seat at a nicer table that a young couple left. Edwin went to get their coffees and apple scones.

Jordan slid into a chair next to her. She realized he was following her car this morning. There was a reason she felt strange while driving the freeway. He knew the stores she and Geri shopped.

Gloria didn't react but said the first thing her brain could put together. She was glad their packages were in the car which was in the parking ramp. Jordan lost them for a while and then saw them cross the street. Edwin was very tall and hard to miss in his red shirt and black slacks.

"I thought you were on a cruise."

"The cruise was only for two weeks upstate. I'm upset about the police patrolling where I live. I followed you to deliver my message in person. Stay out of my life and my parent's house."

The bodyguard deposited the hot coffee and wrapped scones on the table. He leaned over and talked to Jordan.

"When I was at your home, I peeked around the corner and noticed your pool lights weren't on. I could see the bulb casing was corroded from greasy slime. Electrocution is a terrible way to go. If I were you, I'd run home and get your shit fixed."

Jordan's face got red, and he left the shop.

Edwin opened his coffee and stirred in the extra cream and sugar. He opened his scone and smeared three patties of butter on top. He was about to take a bite when he looked at Gloria. There was no butter left. He went over to the counter and brought her two butter packets.

"Next time, I shoot him."

Gloria took a sip of the hot liquid. She was thinking about the same thing. She took the plastic knife and cut her scone in half. Gloria slid the other half and a butter packet to Edwin.

"I'll be on your side at the witness stand. Self-defense might work or helping a damsel in distress might be better."

Edwin smiled.

27 Vermont Location

Their plane landed in Burlington, Vermont, and the baggage was collected. Rory looked around. Edwin disappeared into the restroom.

"Dillon must be late. We need to wait here, or we can find a restaurant in the airport."

Gloria voted for the restaurant idea. He texted Dillon about their new meeting location.

After eating hamburgers, Dillon arrived to collect the travelers. Rory stood up and shook Dillon's hand. He introduced Edwin, the bodyguard.

"I'm glad to see everyone. Sorry about being late. There was an exceptionally long line of lumber trucks in my way."

They piled into the van the movie company rented.

"Our location for filming is a rental home off East Lakeshore Drive. The view of Malletts Bay is spectacular. We'll be doing the dialogue and fake romantic stuff there. Our dancing will take place in New York City. The company didn't like the security at the warehouse that was available here. Hence, the reason for the venue change. We're only going to be here three weeks or less per our director. Gloria and I will try to do the scenes correctly the first time."

"Great. The sooner we go back home, the better," said Rory as he looked at his wife.

"We have two trailers here for costume changes, and they've put us in rooms on the same floor at the hotel. The rooms are normal stuff. Gloria and

Rory's rooms are the best ones. Edwin will be staying with me when he's not watching Gloria."

Dillon parked the van. Gloria walked around the movie set and looked at the bedroom set. She hoped Rory would be all right with the scenes taken during the evening. He agreed not to hang around the set. She was going to be self-conscious enough.

They looked out the living room window and liked the view. There was a large porch with comfortable chairs and tables. A small fireplace was on one side.

"This fireplace is cool. How do we light the logs?" asked Gloria.

Dillon went to a small box by the patio door and flipped a switch. The gas log lit. They wouldn't need to worry about soot. After the house tour, they checked the trailers.

Heading to their hotel, they dropped off the luggage. The group walked to a nearby pizza joint. The men ordered two supreme pizzas with extra meat. Gloria ordered the veggie pizza. Soft drinks were chosen because the filming started at six in the morning to catch the sunrise in the background.

Breakfast would be catered, and a company would have box lunches for meals at the site. In the second week, a food truck would arrive.

Having filmed before, Gloria knew how the equipment worked as did Dillon. However, she was disappointed when he lost his concentration. Dillon stumbled on a few of his lines. They reshot the scenes.

The first week of filming went okay, and they were on schedule.

On the weekend, they drove to a cabin and stayed. The two men went fishing. Gloria and Rory went for long walks.

The second week of filming was the love scenes and bedroom shots. Rory drove into town and went to the local museum and finally the library. After the first day, he grew quiet and didn't ask her about the filming. The next day was one of the bedroom scenes. Rory looked worried.

Gloria went to her husband.

"The scene with Dillon will be fine. We've danced close to each other. He's lifted me by my crotch, so there shouldn't be any difficulties. I love you, but you aren't helping me by getting jealous."

"I'm not jealous of Dillon. Although I will regret those words if the film shows the two of you getting hot."

"Trust me, I can fake hot."

Rory suddenly started laughing. His wife was full of disguises.

"At least you don't fake hot with me."

Gloria knew Rory would be all right.

"Why don't you hang around our hotel room? It would be more comfortable than the library."

Rory kissed her and watched Gloria leave.

The bedroom scene was shot four times. The film crew wanted to get all sorts of angles. She wore a soft silk slip with lace running down the front in strategic places.

Dillon wore tight-fitting underwear. After moving the sheets and her slip, they did their lines and barely moved their bodies. At the end of the day, both were tired. They put their robes on and sat outside drinking bottles of water.

"I thought being with you in bed would be fun and romantic."

Gloria smiled.

"The film crew was very distracting. My body feels tortured. I'd rather dance."

"Me, too."

Dillon looked at the water.

"Sometimes I wonder if Rory hadn't come along, we might have been an item."

Gloria didn't know how to respond. Her stomach growled from not eating lunch.

"I'm hungry. Let's change and go back to the hotel."

Edwin Sherman was waiting for her as she exited the house. He didn't say anything to the two quiet actors.

The other love scenes were easier. They weren't in bed.

The final scene was done. They were already outside.

"Let's go for a walk," suggested Dillon.

"A short walk is all I can handle."

They walked the beach. Edwin followed a short distance. Dillon forgot she brought her bodyguard.

"Edwin is very protective."

"Yes, we're good friends. We share butter and scones."

Dillon picked up a rock and threw it over the water.

"I enjoyed kissing you."

"Dillon, I'm married unless you've forgotten."

He sighed.

"I'm very aware of those facts. I just wanted to let you know. You dance better than you kiss."

Gloria hit him.

"Ow! Your hands are strong."

"Dillon, you must be in between women to start picking on me. Find someone to date and quickly, please."

"You are right. I miss Geri and Bella. You are the next person on my closest friend list."

"Good, I like you as a friend, period. Let's keep things that way. End of discussion. Now can we go back?"

They turned and almost ran into Edwin. The three went back to the hotel. Their part of the filming was complete. They could stay or check out of the hotel.

In the morning, Gloria, Rory, and Edwin flew home. Gloria would have three weeks off until the filming started in New York City.

When they arrived at their apartment, Rory was depositing the luggage. Their door was open. The elderly neighbor's orange female tabby cat snuck into their apartment. Rory closed the door.

They were in bed when the cat decided to join them.

"What was that thing?"

Rory turned on the light. Sitting at the foot of the bed was the regal cat. She meowed softly.

"Mara, kitty, not again. She's been doing this lately. Usually, it's in the morning before I go to the gym. She probably wondered where I've been."

Rory put on his robe, picked up the cat, and knocked on their neighbor's door. Gloria waited with their door open. The woman's daughter came out to talk with them. Her mother was moving into a nursing home, and she was looking to place the cat with a family.

Rory and Gloria went back to bed. Gloria turned on the light. Rory sat up.

"You want to keep Mara?"

"Yes."

"Good, now we can get some sleep. You let her know tomorrow."

"Thank you."

Rory was already asleep. Gloria wiggled her feet in delight.

"We have a cat!"

In the morning, a package arrived after Rory left. Edwin would take the day off because Gloria was staying home. There were new, more secure locks on her doors.

She opened the package. Inside the box was a marble female mouth partially open. The object was very sexy.

"Dillon. Heavens, this won't work in this apartment. Rory would flip a gasket."

The marble object was cute. She thought about Dillon's kisses.

"No, we don't keep the gift."

She wrapped the item in the box and secured the top with tape.

"This will look good at my father's place. We can put the lips in the men's restroom. We might have to secure it with bolts first. I think a person can drill marble. Stan will know. An innovative idea, Gloria."

28 Mara

The elderly woman's daughter helped Gloria bring the cat's carry cage, water, food dishes, cat food, litter pan, and leash to Rory's apartment.

Once the items were stowed away, she placed the food and water in the kitchen and the litter pan in the bathtub. The cat explored the apartment again.

"See, Mara, you've been here before except now we have your food and potty. This will be your new home. When Rory and I go on vacation, Stan and his wife volunteered to take care of you."

Gloria grabbed a book she wanted to read. The book was newly published and was written by a female dancer. Her hot cup of tea was next to her chair. The cat curled up on her lap.

For lunch, Gloria opened a small plastic container of yogurt. She went to get the frozen blueberries out of the freezer. When she turned, the cat was on the counter licking the yogurt.

"I guess a little yogurt never hurt anyone, but half a container is all for now."

She put the lid on and wrote in black marker pen, *cat*. Grabbing another container for herself, she opened her jar and put the berries on top. The cat didn't like the berries and jumped off the counter.

Rory called and wanted to know how her day was going.

"Our cat likes yogurt."

"Not to worry, I'll pick some more when I stop at the store on my way home. If I buy a cooked chicken, do we have any macaroni for a salad?"

"Yes, get some mayonnaise, celery, and peppers. A medium head of lettuce would be nice. See if they have cat shaky toys at the store."

"I'm writing this down. Have a fun day reading."

Gloria went back to her book. It seemed strange to have some free time for herself. She kept debating if she should tell Rory about her present. She decided against the idea.

"Edwin believed something was going on between her and Dillon. There wasn't. But how do I acknowledge the gift."

She got up and looked at the box. The box was shipped priority, so there was a tracking number given to the recipient.

"No need to acknowledge the lips. He can check online."

Her cat meowed in agreement.

"You're a smart cat."

Rory came home. She chopped the vegetables and placed them in a bowl. He helped her with the lettuce and the plates. While the noodles were draining, she mixed the mayonnaise into the vegetables. The cooled noodles were added. She dished the salad into the lettuce cups and cut the chicken.

Gloria looked at her husband with Mara. Mara was tucked by his side. She brought over her husband's plate of food, and they ate.

When they went to bed, the cat plopped down between the two of them. Rory picked up the cat, rubbed her head gently, and put her outside the bedroom, and closed the door.

He came back to bed and crawled in next to her.

"This is better. I have plans for you that require immediate contact."

Gloria smiled. Later, she would open the door and let Mara back into bed.

In the morning, Edwin arrived with a bag full of cat toys. They let the cat select a toy and hid the rest in a kitchen cupboard.

Upon arriving home later in the day, they saw all the cat toys strewn over the living room carpet. The cardboard was chewed on the toys still attached. Mara found a way inside the cupboard to retrieve her presents.

Edwin and Gloria watched the cat open the cupboard door to see if she missed anything. Rory opened the apartment door with a huge cart. He brought in two pieces of a cat tower.

"I see Mara has been spreading the cheer all over our living room. I arrived with this tower in the nick of time. The sales clerk told me there were only four bolts. Putting the tower into one piece should be simple."

Rory threw the manual on the table. Edwin and Rory put the bolts on and righted the tower. The cat jumped up the carpeted steps, The cat tower fell over lopsided.

Gloria intervened.

"I can see by the manual that the bolts are on upside down."

Rory and Edwin grinned.

"Men take the shortcut to four. Like the song, Gloria's, 1,2,3,4, the steps should be followed.

"We sing the song differently," mentioned Rory.

"Really. I bet it's Gloria's and 4."

"Nope, G's and 4."

Gloria hit her husband in his right arm.

"Ouch. Why are dancers strong?"

Gloria looked at the two men and snuggled with Mara until the men fixed the cat tower. She put the cat at the top. The cat looked at the men and immediately jumped down.

"See, now Mara has trust issues. Females are intelligent."

The men outsmarted the cat. They put her favorite mouse on the top. Mara leaped two steps and settled in the top carpeted box.

"For a minute there, I thought we would have to return the tower." Edwin petted the soft cat.

"Nice, kitty."

He picked the shaky toy off the floor and pulled off the rest of the wrapper. Edwin gave Rory the toy. Rory played with Mara while Gloria fixed supper.

Edwin waved, took the cart back to the elevator, and left.

29 Filming in New York City

The dancers assembled at the movie company's studio to begin filming the dance scenes. Gloria waited in the wings until they wanted her to start. Dillon stepped beside her.

"You didn't tell me whether you liked my gift."

"I did. The lips are secured to the men's bathroom next to the urinal at my father's bistro."

"Ouch, you are really bad, Gloria. I should have bought the cheap plaster of Paris except they didn't have the same impact."

"Um, I think that's my entrance cue."

Gloria moved slowly toward her marker on the floor. The spotlight was blinding, so she shut her eyes briefly. The dark was her friend, and she began her dance.

Dillon watched her along with Edwin. Edwin spoke.

"I never get tired of seeing her move those legs. My daughter is five years old. I showed her Gloria's picture. My wife was commanded by my daughter to go buy tights and the netting thing."

Edwin ruined the moment for Dillon. He liked watching Gloria dance.

"It's called a tutu if it's short. Usually, little girls don't wear a longer and more romantic dress until they are older."

"Really, how strange. The long dress is called romantic. But I guess you should know. Do you think Gloria would show my little girl a few steps?"

154

"I'm sure she would. I've got a book my sister read when she was your daughter's age. I'll ask her to send you the copy."

"Gee, thanks, man."

Edwin typed his phone and address in Dillon's phone.

Dillon left the area. He wasn't dancing until an hour later.

The filming lasted three months because the dancers were given additional days off, so the scenery could be changed. Dillon and Gloria finished their dances together and their final scenes.

They met at a restaurant for seafood to celebrate. There were thirty dancers and other actors, and the place was noisy. Rory stayed by Gloria's side all evening. Edwin drove them home and picked his car up at their place.

The opening night was scheduled for two months away.

30 Peeping Tom

A new neighbor moved into the apartment across from Rory and Gloria's apartment. She was told by their security people that the single man was a news reporter. Gloria wasn't excited to meet the man. She wanted to step away from the spotlight for a few weeks and do her normal routine.

She went to the gym and her dance studio. Next was a haircut. By the time Gloria and Edwin returned home, it was four o'clock in the afternoon.

He checked the apartment locks and left her door. He saw the door across from Gloria's was partially open. Edwin walked to the elevator and stepped inside. The elevator went down two floors. He punched the stop button.

"The door should have been shut. The man was watching Gloria's door. The question is why?"

He looked at the floor light and punched the next stop. Edwin decided to take the stairs. When he reached Gloria's floor, he quietly opened the floor door. He saw a man looking through Gloria's peephole.

Edwin took his phone out and began recording a video. He looked at his watch. Watching the man, he noticed his hands were trying her lock. Then Edwin saw a mechanism sometimes used to open a door. He stopped filming and called the apartment's security people.

The apartment security talked to the man. He went back to his door, went inside, and slammed it shut. Edwin made himself visible to the apartment security man and asked him a bunch of questions about Gloria's neighbor. He rode down in the elevator with the guard to the main apartment office and complained about the tenant.

Edwin reached his car and decided to go back. He stopped a floor short and repeated the drill. The man was again standing outside Gloria's door. Edwin drew his gun and palmed it in his hands.

"Hey, shit for brains, we're going to talk inside your apartment."

Edwin let the man see his gun.

"Don't rob me. I don't have much cash."

Edwin and the man stepped inside his apartment. Edwin left his foot in the door. The man backed away.

"Your name is Randy Ruffin, and you work for a news company. My suggestion about how you run your business isn't important. However, there are choices to decide. Number one is that you quietly move out of this building tomorrow, or else I'm going to send your boss a nice video of a peeping tom. This peeping tom also has a device for breaking into an apartment. My second choice would be to send a copy to the police. Then, thirdly, I can encourage my clients to take legal action against you."

"You can't threaten me, Mr. Sherman."

"Surprise, surprise, you know my name. Why would you learn my name? Guess what else might be a grand surprise? You are wrong. I can threaten you. I'm a security guard. I see the first three choices aren't having an impact."

Edwin grabbed the man and shoved him against the wall. The man's nose started to bleed.

"This is your fourth and last choice. If I haven't changed your mind, there's a final one."

Edwin dropped his hand.

"I'm going to contact my friends."

The threat didn't have any effect on Edwin.

"I don't think you will be doing that move."

Randy looked at the gun that was now visibly laying on his nose. He swallowed.

"I would choose the first choice and move."

"You mean you would shoot me?"

Edwin laughed.

"No way. I would have my friends shoot you. I believe at last count, there were twenty men. They have bigger guns than mine. The bullet load was fifteen, but they bought the kind that holds thirty. Or is the number thirty-two. Yeah, I've got the number right. How many friends do you have? I'll bet none."

Randy whined, "I'll lose my deposit."

Edwin reached in his shirt pocket and threw a one-hundred-dollar bill at the man.

"I'm feeling generous for the moment. Tomorrow, all those feelings will be gone. I'll be stopping at your door in the morning."

The next day a small rental mover truck was near the elevator.

Edwin rode the elevator to his client's floor and was about to knock. Rory stepped out.

"Hello, Edwin, you're a little early. Gloria needs about fifteen more minutes."

"Good, if you have some time, I need your help."

Rory looked at Edwin.

"There's been trouble?"

Edwin walked with Rory to the stairway and showed him the video. Rory was angry. Edwin blocked the door.

"I've handled the situation. The man is moving out this morning. He didn't want to meet my twenty men friends who own guns with major bullets."

Rory stepped back.

"Edwin, I like the way you think."

Edwin laughed.

"I've been doing this job since I was eighteen. This jerk is nothing."

The two men made sure the man and his rental truck were gone. Edwin sent the videos anyway. He sent a copy to the apartment manager and Rory. Rory sent the video and the man's name to his lawyer to get a restraining order.

Rory went to his door and kissed his wife goodbye a second time. He told her their nosy reporter moved out.

Gloria looked at her husband and the bodyguard. She noticed Edwin's strap on his gun was unbuckled. She could put two and two together.

"If I see the man again in the future, how do I proceed?"

"Our lawyer will handle the man. He's probably working the problem as we speak," smiled Rory.

"He was bad?"

"Mr. Ruffin crossed the line. Once the news media finds out about him and our swift actions, they will be more careful who they hire. Call this our first test run."

"The price of fame is high. You will be noticed," reminded Edwin.

Rory held his wife and kissed her quickly. She knew they somehow saved her from a possible bad article and a bad reporter.

31 Opening Night

Gloria and Rory stood in the line for the diplomats and important film people. Their hands were sore from shaking many ballet enthusiasts.

Rory was in his tuxedo, and Gloria wore a dark blue velvet gown with high slits and clear heels with rhinestones. Edwin also was in his tuxedo and stood behind them. Dillon and some of the major dancers were on the other side of the room.

The movie theatre was packed with expensive outfits and the cream crop of high society.

She tried to warn her husband about some of the scenes, so he wouldn't react too badly when he saw them in the film. The film was edited to show romantic scenes to enhance the story. He told her that he was a reasonable man.

Finally, the time came for the guests to sit down and watch the movie. Gloria sat with her husband.

He watched her dance a modern routine with some girl dancers. Although barefoot, their dance movements were strong and impressive. The next scene was the male version with bare torsos.

Rory watched the love scenes and grabbed Gloria's hand. He remembered her conversation about faking love. He became a little uncomfortable with the bedroom scene.

Rory whispered in her ear. "Good photography, especially with the sheets."

Gloria let out her breath.

"The next scene is my three costume changes. There's the black fur, next is the red satin, and the final leopard outfit."

She danced only with the men. Rory received the same treatment and danced only with the women.

There were more scenes of the two major players dancing alone and then together at practice. The book was a love story about two young dancers who made the big time.

Dillon and Gloria danced with the other dancers. This dance was more powerful and showed their skills as jumpers.

"I have to admit, this scene is beautiful."

Gloria squeezed his hand.

"This part and dance are the best in the movie. The ending scene will bring tears to women's eyes."

The moderator told the story because there was only the soft music:

> *The male dancer cheats. He comes to her practice session to tell her goodbye. Instead, the man watches backstage through a shredded sheer curtain.*
>
> *She wears her white ballet dancer skirt which reaches mid-calf. The skirt has only two thin layers between her bodysuit. The white under-bodysuit is cut low. The song is slow and passionate.*
>
> *At first, the audience sees glimpses of the female dancer through the veiled curtain. The camera switches and looks down at her as*

she pirouettes her final dance. This dance is flawless motion.

The male dancer tells himself she is too perfect.

He exits and doesn't tell the beloved female dancer goodbye. They will never meet again.

Her hand and leg pause in mid-air. She realizes he's not coming and stops. She leaves the stage forever.

In the movie, the camera focused on Dillon's expression outside the dance building one last time.

Rory didn't like what he saw. Rory believed Dillon was in love with his wife.

Gloria squirmed as if she was uncomfortable with the scene. She glanced at Rory.

He didn't look at her. The theatre lights glowed back on. The movie was over. Rory gave his hand to Gloria.

"Not so much of a tragedy."

They stood in the reception line and again shook hands with people. There was a lull in people coming through the line.

"I must use the ladies' restroom."

Edwin escorted Gloria to her bathroom break. Dillon walked over to Rory.

"What did you think of the movie?"

Rory thought a minute.

"The movie was nicely filmed and choreographed. I would call the movie a hit, but then I'm a little prejudiced. My wife made the movie great."

Dillon made a move to leave. Rory grabbed his arm.

"Don't send my wife any more presents."

Dillon shook off Rory's arm. He saw a few dignitaries watching.

"I told Gloria her dancing was better than her kisses."

Rory also saw the dignitaries walking their way.

Dillon only had a few moments.

"I lied."

Dillon walked away.

Rory was going to go after him when he saw Gloria was back in the large room.

Edwin stood beside Rory.

"I wouldn't hit him today, sir. Maybe next time would be better without ladies present."

Gloria approached the two men. There seemed to be a lot of tension in the room.

"I talked with Mr. Chadsworth. We are free to leave."

Rory turned and took his startled wife in his arms and gave her a long, lingering kiss.

Dillon stomped out of the room. Rory smiled.

"I'm ready."

Edwin wore a happy look on his face as they left. Rory showed some balls.

32 Full Disclosure

The travel destination brochures were on the table when Rory came home. They needed a vacation to celebrate the movie. He sorted through them and selected three that he would like to visit.

The cat was at the veterinarian with a bad ear infection and would stay the night.

Rory felt now was the time to talk with Gloria about starting a family. He waited two weeks for her to rejuvenate herself after all the publicity regarding the film.

He fixed them both drinks and sat down in the living room. Edwin dropped off Gloria and left.

"Sit down. We need to talk about starting a family. You can stop taking birth control pills, or whatever it is that you are currently using."

Gloria knew this day would come. Her father warned her not to wait. Her secret would need to be revealed. She sat down and took a long sip.

"Remember when I told you about my car accident at age eighteen?"

"Yes, your boyfriend, Jordan, was driving the car, and you couldn't dance for a year."

Gloria walked to the patio door. She went back in time and relived the accident and aftermath in fifteen seconds. She turned white.

Rory looked at his wife with concern. He knew there was more to the accident.

"Gloria?"

She turned and sat on the ottoman.

"At the time, I was pregnant and lost my baby."

"I'm sorry. Losing a child that young is terrible."

She sighed.

"There's more to the story."

Rory guessed.

"You haven't been taking any contraceptives? But you do take medicine."

"Yes, I do take other female stuff. After the accident, they tried several types of medicine to stop the bleeding. None of them worked. I had an excellent doctor who performed a laparoscopic hysterectomy. There was minimal scarring on the outside. However, the inside isn't there to help produce or carry a child."

Rory wanted to tell his wife he understood. However, he didn't.

"Why, Gloria? When were you going to tell me? The important thing is you didn't. I married you while believing I would become a father someday."

She went to her desk and pulled out a folder.

"You can be a father. There are ways."

Now Rory was angry.

"You're unbelievable. I can't do this right now. I'm staying at the office tonight. Tomorrow we talk."

He grabbed his briefcase and left the apartment. Gloria finished her drink. She sat for a long time on the ottoman.

"You were right."

She knew his pride was hurt and his trust. Her husband was not at fault. She was.

166

Gloria didn't know how to correct the situation. There was no reason to call anyone. She was all alone with her dilemma. At that moment, she hated herself and Jordan.

She sat on their bed doing her breathing exercises. Gloria closed her eyes. The familiar darkness arrived. The dark centered her well-being, usually.

"Breathe in, breathe out, breathe in, breathe out."

She gave up. The dark wasn't working. The exercise wasn't calming her down. Her head was spinning. She felt ice cold.

A long time ago, the car spun out of control before coming to a stop. She kept living the accident over and over the first year after it happened. She shivered.

Her current stress with Rory triggered the event repeatedly in her brain. Her therapist told Gloria the mind liked to play tricks on a person. She could stop the swirling motion.

Gloria grabbed an Afghan to warm herself. She closed her eyes again.

"I can stop the spin. You can do this."

She mentally pushed sad thoughts from her brain. Her thoughts must be positive. This was the only way she knew how to take control.

Gloria watched the car come around in her mind. She saw her face in the side mirrors. The face was older. She was no longer eighteen. She blinked away the scene.

"I'm alive, and I'll be fine. Rory needs some time alone is all. He loves me."

She tried to sleep.

Gloria tossed and turned. The Afghan was too hot. She was miserable. Her brain was still firing. She remembered Geri's comment.

"Miserable people belong in opera, not ballet."

She went to the refrigerator to get some yogurt. She held the door open to cool herself. A milk product would help her go back to sleep. She dropped some frozen blueberries into the carton of yogurt. Finding some pecans, she crumbled a few on top. She would make fruit and nut granola in the morning.

Gloria stumbled back to her bed. Rory liked her granola. They could do coffee in the morning and talk. She wanted to talk with him about everything. Now that he knew her secret, they could build their life together.

"How do I fix this mess if he doesn't come around?"

Rory would need to understand.

The serious health consequence after what happened to her in her prior life was there. She had lived with the accident damage for years. The accident wasn't her fault. She couldn't worry about her past. There was only the future.

A future baby could happen whenever they were ready. She hoped Rory felt the same way. The two of them would be good for a child. Rory would protect their child, and she would defend the child's every move.

She dumped the empty yogurt carton in the trash. The spoon was put in the dishwasher. She waited. There was hope in her heart that her husband would return. She listened for his presence.

A final look outside at the fog rolling into the area, she decided it was time to turn in. Gloria missed Mara's pitter-patter and meow. There was no one to hug.

At midnight, she gave up. Gloria punched the lights off and went to bed.

About two in the morning, she heard a sound and awakened. Her eyes flashed open. Gloria couldn't remember if she locked the doors. She thought she did but might have forgotten to push the slide across.

Slowly getting out of bed, her cell phone was placed in her pajama top pocket. She opened her bedside table. The gun and flashlight were in her hands. She heard another sound. Their building didn't have rats.

Crawling on the floor, she moved into the hallway. Her eyes adjusted to the dark. A small nightlight in the guest bathroom helped. There was no one there.

Gloria thought about texting Rory. The phone would light up. She was to the corner of the hall and the kitchen. Gloria thought to herself.

"Rory has returned."

Gloria was about to stand up and reveal herself. She heard what sounded like an icicle dropping. She stood up thinking the person in the apartment must be Rory.

There was another sound. She knew this sound. Water was falling into a cup. Rory would turn the kitchen lights on to get a glass of ice water. The person in their apartment was not her husband.

She stepped around the corner and saw a figure in the dark. The stove light silhouetted the man's shape.

Gloria clicked the flashlight on with her left hand and pointed the gun with her right. The vision in front of her registered. The man wore a dark face mask, and he carried a gun with a silencer. She dropped the flashlight and immediately fired twice.

Gloria was a trained firearms person. She knew where to shoot to stop someone cold in their tracks. She picked the gut and lung. The man swore and dropped to the floor.

Hitting the kitchen light switch, she dialed for their apartment security. The man came quickly and saw the intruder on the floor bleeding. He dialed the emergency number for the police.

Gloria went over to the masked man. He tried to talk. She knew who the man was. His voice confirmed her suspicion.

"Jordan?"

The man couldn't talk.

"Why did you break into my home? Oh, my god, you killed Geri and Bella."

The man opened his mouth to speak. He croaked out two words.

"Only Geri."

The masked man passed out.

170

The police and ambulance came. They carried Jordan out on a stretcher.

The police were going to question her when Gloria stumbled.

She looked at her hand holding her shoulder. There was blood seeping between her fingers. Her fear and shock subsided. The hot pain was intense. She passed out.

A second ambulance was called and raced to the scene.

The security guard contacted Rory and Edwin.

33 Awakening in the Hospital

There were lights in the ceiling when Gloria awakened. The clock read five-thirty. She didn't know if it was morning or night. She tried to move, and her left arm hurt. She was bandaged with lots of white gauzes. She smelled antiseptic and alcohol.

Rory opened his eyes when he heard his wife groan. He came by her bedside.

"You've been shot, Gloria, in the arm. The doctor told me the wound will heal. Don't worry. You will be able to dance. Let me get you some water."

She took a sip and looked at him. He took her cold hands and tried to kiss them warmer.

"I shouldn't have left you alone. I'm sorry."

She shook her head.

"I don't remember the door. There was a flashback of the car spinning. I couldn't sleep and heard a noise. I took out the gun and went to the kitchen. There was a mask. I fired."

"The door was locked, but the slide wasn't. Jordan is in the hospital. He won't be going far from the police escort. He can barely walk from the two shots you fired. Because he fired at you, it's self-defense. You did well to keep your cool and self-control. I'm enormously proud of you. So are your father and Stan."

She laid in the hospital bed vulnerable.

Her eyelids flipped.

Rory knew his wife was back with the living. Her ability to float in and out was remarkable. He saw her grow stronger as she realized where she was.

172

Gloria looked at her surroundings and vaguely remembered. Then Jordan's words hit her.

"Jordan told me that he only killed Geri. Bella's killer is still out in the world."

Rory was impressed.

"I'm glad you are with us. Your dad talked with his police friend. Jordan admitted to wanting to kill you at age eighteen. He didn't want the baby. His diary found at the house reflected his demented thoughts. Geri found his diary and read about his evil plan with the car. She threatened to reveal the attempted murder. You also saw the small red book. He believed you might have read his diary or part of the book. His need to eliminate you from this earth overtook his warped obsession. That's why he came after you."

Gloria remembered why Rory was not at their apartment. She rolled over away from him.

"I'm here."

Rory stood.

He saw the pain in her eyes.

She shut down and wouldn't talk.

"Gloria, whatever happened is not us. I promise."

Almost losing his wife to a maniac made Rory focus on the importance of his world. Gloria was more important than a child.

"I talked with your father some about pride. He said there was one time in his life that he wished he could erase his pride. For him, the error was too late. Your mom wouldn't ever return. I don't want us to make the same mistake."

Rory bent over and whispered in her ear, "*Te amo, mi amor.*"

Gloria slowly smiled. He always whispered those words to her. She turned over. She spoke the words for him.

"I love you, my love."

"We'll talk more when you get home. Right now, I don't want to have children. I only want us and Mara. Gloria, I love you."

Gloria yawned. The events were too much. The nurse came in to help her to the bathroom. Her arm was pounding. She took her medicine and fell almost asleep.

"Rory?"

"I'm here."

Rory watched his wife. She drifted finally into a deep sleep. He wasn't going anywhere until Edwin relieved him.

In a couple of days, Gloria went home.

Jordan was convicted, sentenced, and put in prison for murder and attempted murder. She remembered Geri telling her to stay away from Jordan. Geri saw the real person that existed. Per Jordan, Gloria's mother knew about the diary.

"No wonder Geri practically lived at our home. Her father traveled a lot. When he was gone, Geri would make excuses to stay overnight. Geri was like a sister and another daughter to the Strand family. She was protected in our home."

Gloria and Rory took a week's vacation and drove to Atlantic City where they first explored their relationship.

No further mention was made about having a family. Gloria could rest easy while her arm healed. They ate corn dogs on the beach. Rory bought her a book about Trojan horses. They gambled a little.

When they returned from vacation, they started reviewing new condominium complexes for sale with a better security system.

34 Christmas Dancers

The weather turned brisk and started to lightly snow. Edwin escorted Gloria to the ballet Christmas rehearsal. She could dance with the royal ballet for the play with the sugar plum fairy.

The ballet company was not the same one where Dillon worked. Rory made sure Gloria checked before applying for the position.

She did find out that Dan was on the company's permanent payroll. She was delighted to see him at practice. They hugged each other.

"I didn't know you worked here. What an excellent job to capture for your portfolio!"

Dan looked well and happy.

"My job here is wonderful. The company pays me a nice sum for the truly brief period that we perform. I've been here since I left Johnny Zander."

"Ugh, he was a terrible person. The man tried to sue me for not dancing in a movie that contained his book as a script. The judge threw out the case."

"I heard the same thing from my sources and that's why I apologized for his bad behavior. I'm sorry we ever met this person and writer. You and Rory are still together. Impressive job on the second movie. You blew me away. I wasn't impressed with Dillon at the opening ceremonies. He seemed quite full of himself."

Gloria shook her head. "I saw him change as a person. I'm not sure his life is going too well on a personal level."

"I hated seeing the female dancers fall for his lines."

Gloria was going to change the subject when the coordinator came into the dance room. They were given their program and costumes. Tomorrow, they would start practice. She handed the pile of clothes to Edwin to carry to their vehicle. He complained about the mouse costume. The head kept flopping in his face.

Gloria took a selfie of the two of them and would post it to her website when she arrived home.

At the last minute, they stopped at her father's place. She went into the restroom and noticed the marble lips were in the female's bathroom. Her father told her, there were too many male business cards left in the mouth of the statue in the male restroom.

She hugged her dad and showed him the mouse head. He didn't like the nose. Gloria put the head on the wood counter near the taps. Stan didn't see the head until he turned around. He dropped the glass he was going to fill on the floor.

Gloria watched him sweep the glass in a bin and dump the contents in the garbage.

"That is by far the ugliest mouse head I've ever seen. The colors are garish," commented Stan as he touched the head.

"He looks better under the overhead lights."

"Well, I'm going to sit in the back row then while you're wearing this getup."

Her father poured himself an orange juice. His doctor told him only one cup of coffee a day.

"I'll be right beside you."

177

Edwin came inside after parking the car.

"The dance hall today at practice looked like a freak show, but I'm sure my daughter will love the play. We've been reading her the sugarplum story. She likes the weird mouse."

Gloria smiled.

"See, little kids will like me."

Stan refilled a new glass of pop and sat down. He was on his break.

"They will like you because kids don't know any better."

Edwin told them his daughter was getting excited about the play, and she could now pirouette without falling over.

They said their goodbyes, and Gloria was taken home.

The mouse costume was dropped on the large island. The cat jumped up on the island, saw the mouse head, took a swipe at the head, and ran around the living room like a maniac cat. That's when Rory came home. He saw the mouse's head.

"Poor puffball. Did that ole big mouse scare you?"

Rory snuggled and petted the cat.

Gloria took the head and dumped it in the closet with the costumes. There was a slight scratch on the plastic nose and a whisker was missing from the mouse head. Gloria threw the busted whisker in the trash.

"What about pour Gloria?"

Rory kissed his wife. He put the cat down.

"Tough day, I see. How was Dan?"

"Strange day is a better word. Dan looks great. He is still thin but is doing well. The ballet company has been a respectable job for him. Low stress and hours. I've ordered our group tickets. Both Edwin and Stan's daughters are excited to see the Christmas play."

"I'm just as excited. I've never seen you in fake fur except for the very real black fox fur from the movie. The fake fur might be an interesting change."

She gave her husband the evil eye.

"Don't you dare laugh at my performance!"

Rory liked teasing her.

"I'll let the kids start laughing first."

She picked up a piece of the cheese she was carving.

"No, no, not the cheese. I give up."

Gloria came over and stuffed a slice in his mouth. He broke off a piece to give to the cat. The cat stuck her nose up at the cheese.

"Maybe she likes Swiss cheese better or what's that stinky cheese called?"

Now Gloria was getting irritated.

"Limburger!"

She crushed the cracker and handed the crumbs to Rory.

"What's with the crumbs?"

She went to the refrigerator. There wasn't much inside for food.

"They are your supper."

Rory sighed. He found the magnet on the refrigerator and dialed the number for the pizza place. He looked at her for which type.

179

She laughed smugly, "I'll take extra cheese pizza."

He ordered her vegetarian instead which was her usual. They waited until the pizza arrived and sat at the kitchen island.

"The realtor called me today. She has found a condominium that might work for us. Is there a day and time that you are available for a preview?"

He passed her the real estate description. Gloria knew the area. The condominium was in a nicer part of town and close to the freeway. It was about five miles from their current apartment.

"Saturday in the afternoon will work. My pizza is good."

35 Sugarplum Ballet

Gloria saw her guests sitting in the front row off to the left side. She waved. Rory saw her and waved back. He held up his four fingers like mouse ears. She gritted her teeth snarling back at him.

The two little girls were wedged between their fathers, Edwin, and Stan. They watched the curtain for the magical opening. Gloria thought briefly how nice if they and Rory could have children.

Rory saw Gloria's moment of despair before she turned away.

"Excuse me a moment, I need to go backstage to make sure the other security guard is there watching Gloria."

Edwin made a move to go with him.

"No, she would want you to stay here. You are now her guests for the evening."

He went through the maze of dancers and found the door with the mouse's face. He nodded to her security guard and knocked. Gloria opened the door and fell into his arms.

"I get weepy at Christmas time."

Rory remembered and said, "I know. There's all the kid stuff."

She nodded.

"You're the prettiest mouse dancer that I've ever seen in silk ballet shoes."

"Oh, no, you shouldn't be able to see my feet. I forgot the special socks."

Rory helped her put them on.

181

"Wow, these are puffy. Go knock them dead, Gloria."

He kissed her for good luck and returned to his seat. Guy looked at Rory.

"She'll be fine. I helped her with the ugly socks."

Gloria's father relaxed as did Stan.

There was another knock on her door. She quickly opened the door believing Rory wanted one more kiss.

She stepped back.

"Dillon, what are you doing here dressed in Dan's costume?"

Dillon shut the door after she waved the okay to her security man.

"I see you still have an armed guard at your side."

He stopped in his tracks and grimaced.

"Oh, Gloria, this is the ugliest mouse costume ever. You were nuts to pick this job. I would have waited for the swan piece. Yes, you would look better with white feathers as a crown on your head. Even black feathers would have been a better choice."

She started to speak.

"No, don't tell me they sold you the bill of goods that the lights will change your costume. They won't."

She looked exasperated and nodded.

Dillon smiled.

"I can see the headlines; movie star makes the ballet but sells herself short. I can't even see your real feet doing en pointe. Your legs look like blankets. There will be no appearance of flight in your grand jete. Oh, I'm sorry, you aren't doing that jump. Can you even pirouette? Look, the plastic crown is even loose. Cheap is a word the audience will use."

Now Gloria was mad. She was getting paid good money to perform. She wanted to hit him and throw her gray fur outfit in his smug face.

"Go disturb some young woman who gives a crap about your thoughts! The crown is supposed to wiggle."

"Ouch. A wiggly cheap crown with rhinestones is unbelievably bad. I saw Rory and your crew in the front row. Those seats are pricey."

"Get out."

"I can't even give you a hug for good luck?"

Gloria threw her makeup jar at him. He caught the jar and placed the weapon on the counter

"The answer is a no. I'm quietly backing out of your dressing room, Ms. Pretty Mouse. See, there's a compliment. Now I'm leaving."

Dillon left, and Gloria didn't know how Rory was going to react to seeing Dillon versus Dan on stage.

"Dan, this was not the time to get the flu. Bad timing."

Gloria watched the production on her computer. She was able to see the live feed. However, she couldn't see her guests.

There was a third knock on her door. She looked at the screen. She wasn't due to perform for ten minutes. She opened the door.

"Rory?"

He looked around her dressing room.

"Dan has the flu. Dillon is the alternate."

Rory crushed his body into hers.

"I know. I don't trust the guy. Can we go home now?" suggested Rory.

Gloria looked at the concern in his eyes.

"Only if you want to disappoint my guests and a whole audience of New York City people. They hate to pay and have their fun canceled. There also could be a little kid riot at not seeing the mouse."

She could see Rory thinking about how to get out of a sticky situation.

Gloria kissed him with all her passion.

Rory relaxed.

"Not fair. I'll hold you to those thoughts when I get you home tonight."

Rory unwillingly returned to his seat.

Gloria waited until the curtain boy told her now was the moment in which she should make her entrance.

She looked at the furry mouse costume and added a white silk scarf. She decided she was going to change the mouse dance.

Wrapping the silk around her neck, she went flying like an ice skater across the expanse of the open stage. The side dancers looked at each other.

Her mouse head flew off, and she quietly picked up the head. Pretending to re-screw the head back on, she next threw the head to the curtain boy.

He wasn't prepared. Startled, he dropped the head and stepped three feet onto the stage to retrieve the mouse's broken crown. The other side dancers swirled around the crown barely missing the curtain boy.

Gloria picked up her scarf and used it with her hands in graceful movements while dancing. Only her port de bras looked like crab arm movements. The audience laughed.

She went to the side of the stage which was part of her program.

While off the stage, she took off the ugly socks because she was too hot. Her cue came to go on, and she danced some more. People noticed the missing socks.

Halfway through the mouse dance, she moved again to the sides and finally took the itchy bottom mouse pants off. She was wearing her bodysuit, leotards, ballet shoes, and the large mouse top.

Encouraged by how much better she felt, her last cue as the mouse creature came. She danced the ending part of her routine.

Rory knew his wife was ad-libbing. She followed the prescribed dance. The little girls in his row went wild with screaming and clapping. The menfolk whistled. The women added to the clapping as encouragement.

Dillon watched Gloria do crazy stuff. He decided to ad-lib because Gloria shouldn't be fired from the ballet company. He would support her in the program change. The overhead lights were killer hot. Her mouse costume was all wrong.

He took his jacket off and threw the cloth to the curtain boy. The jacket hit the boy in the face.

She wiggled like a mouse, and Dillon did the same. He threw his cummerbund to the curtain boy and chased the mouse.

Dillon touched the mouse's arms. Gloria had loosened the nylon tapes. Her mouse arms came off in Dillon's hands. He was surprised and missed a step. Dillon did some more exaggerated fake steps to cover himself.

Then he saw Gloria's evil smile.

"Oh, no, you don't," whispered Dillon to Gloria as he sped past her.

He gave Gloria the next dance sign of what they were going to do with his hand movements.

She nodded.

The mouse and the lead dancer circled the confused other dancers. They met in the middle and Dillon captured the mouse's hand.

He smiled.

Gloria knew he was going to change direction. She switched her leg movements to match his. The mouse's sweet body was twirling into a fouetté.

"Nice circle. Did I tell you sometimes you are fun? We should get back to the program."

Gloria agreed. After the turn, the two dancers followed the trained routine. The rest of the dancers were relieved to continue with the practiced moves.

The crowd loved the interaction between the mouse and the male lead dancer. The audience had no clue regarding the re-programmed dance.

Rory had to give the two dancers credit; the entire Christmas play was now exceptional. Two rows of guests stood up, and the rest of the audience followed.

The owners of the company saw the noisy and excited crowd clapping profusely. They would change the program to accommodate the crowd for the rest of the two-week of shows.

They liked the ending when Gloria invited her two small female friends from her guest row to dance with her for their final bow.

Rory boosted the girls onto the stage floor with Guy's help. She helped the girls' pique and turn. Edwin and Stan took pictures on their cell phones.

The writeups about the sugarplum show sold out the rest of the ticket sales.

Rory came to get Gloria.

"Your dance was the best. I saw immediately how warm you were, and how the two of you dancers changed the movements. Both of you were quick. That takes awesome skills."

"My favorite fan."

The couple went to join the others in their guest party.

On the way home, the two little girls rode together and sang, "Gloria's 1,2,3,4, pique, turn."

Edwin's wife smiled at her husband. He looked at her.

"I love ballet."

Stan and his wife were in the back seat.

"We agree on that score."

Gloria and Rory came home and opened their front door. The cat came over and swiped at her costume top.

"I'm afraid our cat won't ever like this mouse. There goes a button."

Rory picked something out of his pocket. He dropped the realistic object on the floor.

"Oh, no, not a mouse!"

Rory laughed, "It's durable plastic and a chew toy. The kittens at the pet store loved batting the creature."

Mara, their cat went in killer mode.

Gloria saw the look in her husband's eyes.

"How about we dance together. I feel the need to be held by my sweet woman.

"Don't even go there."

"You were the one not playing fair in the dressing room."

Rory took off his jacket and tie. He threw them on the kitchen island.

Gloria looked at her husband and took his hand. They did a slow dance to the music after Rory gave the cylindrical box a voice command for his favorite tune.

"I like the way you act after I've given my best performance."

"I have more ideas after we are done dancing."

"We are at least on the same wave-length."

Rory stopped dancing. They left the cat to her machinations with the rubber mouse.

"Oh, no."

Rory watched his wife scramble to put her entire mouse costume in the closet before Mara went into the second kill position.

Once her costume was safely stored, she turned out the lights.

36 Move to New Condo

She sat on the large island of the empty and newly painted four-bedroom condominium.

"Rory, this unit is beautiful. If we purchased this one, we would have the corner with no neighbors on one side. There's even a washer and dryer in this unit. The only question would be affordability."

Rory looked outside the sixth-floor patio windows toward a small park across the street.

"With the influx of royalties coming from your second movie, we are overqualified. I think we should buy this unit. I liked the three-bedroom but feel we can use the extra room for the exercise equipment and a small studio. I'm five miles closer to my business and we are only that same additional distance from your father's place. I like the ability to get on the freeway or take the subway train."

Gloria went into the master bedroom again. There was room for a small seating area and bookcase library.

"The full-time security guards were on the first floor and the building parking security men are also a plus for us."

Rory stood in the doorway and was excited about the extra room.

Gloria lifted her shoulders.

"Okay, let's contact the realtor and get papers signed."

Within two months, they were all moved. Gloria went down the elevator in their new building to the first floor and retrieved the mail from their mailbox.

Gloria knew Dillon joined a ballet company in Vienna and was no longer with his former company in New York City. Before he left, Dillon told her about a dance opening at his old firm. She sent in her application and video for the job.

There was a letter from the ballet firm. Gloria read the beginning page. They were impressed with her resume but offered the position to a dancer less qualified. Gloria frowned.

She turned to the next page. A key dancer in the second position was retiring. They wondered if she would be interested in accepting. Gloria was to contact them immediately.

She dialed the number and talked with the program director. He loved her mouse routine, previous dancing experience, and her sense of humor. He gave her the amount their company was willing to pay for her services. Gloria would call him back.

Rory's phone immediately answered. Talking with him about the second-position dancer that was available, he was delighted and urged her to accept.

Gloria would start professional ballet practice in a month. Her payroll started immediately. She received the costume company's name to get fitted for several outfits and the shoe company to select five pairs of ballet shoes.

Gloria would go to the ballet company practices and watch the dancers perform. She received the notebook of their scheduled performances which she carried in her briefcase. There were also tapes of the dance routines for her to study in a large carry box at the condominium. Gloria would be kept busy learning about the ballet company's show dances and expectations.

She called her father because he would want to announce to his friends and anyone walking the street outside the front door. He was happy she finally made the top echelon in ballet which was her dream.

Gloria asked him if his friend at the police department knew any further information regarding Bella's murder. Her father was disappointed. He told his daughter there was no further information.

Gloria was puzzled.

She couldn't think of any reason for Bella's death. Bella was the second dancer when she worked for the Columbia Dancing Troupe. The first dancer was her husband, Clark.

"Bella was the first female dancer. Is that the reason she was chosen by some psycho murderer? Where is there a connection?"

She tried to think about the dancers in the troupe. There wasn't anyone who appeared off their rocker, or someone who would hold a grudge.

"She was killed during the day while at her home. Someone must have been watching her for some time to know her routine, or they knew her intimately. The police verified Clark checked into ballet practice."

Gloria was glad Edwin would remain as her bodyguard while she worked for the ballet company. He would be able to handle someone with a knife.

"Clark badged into the ballet practice. He could have used the back door and re-entered later. The problem is no camera, or no one saw him. He went out the back door. How did he get back inside? He used tape, or someone opened the back door and didn't know Clark."

She walked around their new condominium.

"I'm going nuts trying to figure out Bella's murder."

The living room furniture was new. She touched the leather. The cat was fast asleep on the white leather couch and peach wool blanket. Her paws were touching the black velvet pillow.

The Christmas tree was fake green branches and was bare of ornaments. She and Rory decided swinging bulbs would be on the floor the minute they weren't watching their cat. The cat did like to hide under the tree whenever they turned the lights on. She snuggled on the peach velvet tree skirt.

"Maybe I should get one of those tiny barking dogs to put in my gym bag."

The cat came out from behind the couch. She petted Mara.

"Yes, Gloria, the cat would like a barking dog."

The cat disdainfully swished her tail and jumped off the couch.

"I'm going to have to invest in some pepper spray. The ballet company would frown on my large gun on their property. I wonder?"

Gloria thought about Dillon. Was he liking his new job? She envied him. His dream as a dancer was bigger. Men didn't have as much trouble getting into ballet jobs.

"We almost made love before Atlantic City. Then, Rory entered my life. Rory was right to be jealous of Dillon."

She felt relief Dillon was out of the country.

"I need a large crowbar or a stick of dynamite to crack open this case."

37 Wrong Delivery

Rory saw his wife's phone ring. She wasn't in the condominium but was talking to a neighbor down the hall. He answered her phone.

"Mr. Randall here."

"Rory, thank goodness. Is Gloria all right?"

He glanced out their condominium door. He motioned to her.

"Hi, Dillon, how's Vienna?"

Gloria walked back into their condominium. Dillon was confused about her text.

"You sent me a text that something was wrong."

Gloria put her phone on speaker.

"I didn't send you a text."

"Check your phone."

Gloria read the message.

"Wow, my phone was in my bag during ballet practice. I never sent the text. Someone was playing tricks on you and me."

Rory decided to speak up. "Is everything all right with you, Dillon?"

There was a long pause.

"I'm in a little bit of a jam, but there's no need to worry."

Rory looked at Gloria strangely.

"Do you need our help?"

Dillon didn't want to involve them.

"I've got my situation almost covered."

They hung up the call. Gloria didn't know what to think.

"I'll make sure my bag is locked in the future. Also, I better change my login password."

Rory watched her submit the change. He knew the numbers she punched was the date when they met. There was no need to write down the PIN.

The ballet company was on summer break, and her days were less busy. She had been with the ballet company a year and was comfortable with the dancing. She sat down on a high stool at their large island.

"I've been contacting the dancers from the old dance troupe. I wanted their feedback regarding Bella."

Rory wasn't sure about her exploring Bella's former dance friends. However, he was curious.

"Any luck with your questions?"

"One of the women gave me the name of Bella's second cousin. The two women were close."

Rory opened the ham slices and baby Swiss cheese to make their lunch.

"One slice of cheese?" She nodded. Gloria handed him the mustard and relish jar from the refrigerator. She sat down again.

"Close friends do tell each other private thoughts. I assume the cousin told you something."

"She told me Bella was having an affair since the beginning of our tour. Bella wouldn't tell her the man's name. All she said was that he was a dancer."

Rory patted the lettuce in place, smeared mayonnaise, and mustard on the bread. A hefty dollop of her dad's relish was the final addition. He handed her the tall sandwich. He made his sandwich even thicker. She crunched on the delicious sandwich.

"This is delicious. I remember we were all having fun after the shows. You were there for most of the show dates or at least a huge part of them."

Rory finished chewing his bite of sandwich and swallowed.

"I don't recall anyone paying special attention to Bella other than her husband. Let me rethink my thoughts. They weren't exactly lovey-dovey on or off the set. However, I might have been distracted elsewhere. The other dancers joked with Bella like normal. Maybe this distant cousin was wrong about a guy."

Gloria chewed her sandwich and went to the refrigerator. She came back with glasses and the carton. Rory poured the milk.

"Dillon mentioned something once about her. I thought his comment was odd. He said she was hot and a good kisser."

Rory shook his head.

"Dillon talks about all the female dancers that way, including you." He decided not to mention the marble lips and his reaction when Stan told him about the gift's sender.

"I don't think he would want to tangle with a married woman for fear of repercussions."

Gloria knew otherwise.

"Dillon selects any female that he's interested in. I, personally, think there's something wrong with him."

Rory laughed.

"Yes, over-confident, oversexed, and full of his magnetic charisma. He goes out of his way to flirt with the female species. I do have to admit he dances extremely well. His muscles show, and I suppose women like to see the flex."

Gloria wasn't paying attention to their last conversation.

"Hear me out. Let's assume Dillon did have an affair with Bella. There is a possibility something happened. He isn't necessarily a wise person. If this thing happened, why wouldn't he tell the police?"

Her husband thought about the implications.

"The answer would be simple. The man wouldn't want to get involved in a criminal investigation. Dillon would look after his career and himself first. I would guess that he would move away. Your speculation may or may not be true. Without any facts, my detective wife needs to move down the road regarding her theories."

She started to talk. He stopped her.

"Enough, Gloria. No more crazy talk this evening. I need a break. I'm going to watch boring television."

He left her to go into their den.

She was trying to think of a way she could find out more facts when a delivery boy knocked on the door and left a package.

Gloria opened the paper and looked at the plastic bag. There was a clown's wig inside. She looked at the address. There was no return address on the box nor any professional shipping label.

Dillon hated clowns. The package wouldn't be one of his pranks.

Rory told her he needed a break. Her suspicious nature wasn't helping. Gloria decided not to bother her husband. She threw the wig and paper in the garbage can.

"Some clown isn't going to be happy."

38 Parade Hit

Her bodyguard was walking with Gloria down the street in the city. They turned the corner and saw there was a parade coming.

"Let's duck into this jewelry shop until the parade passes."

The sales clerk approached.

"Do you have any inexpensive earrings? Tiny rhinestones for my daughter. She wants to get her ears pierced."

Gloria's eyebrows raised.

The clerk brought back tiny zircon earrings. Edwin paid the clerk, and they exited the store. He put the box in his breast pocket along with a magnetic card with the jeweler's name.

Gloria saw several clowns walk near them. She remembered the strange wig. She looked at the clown's heads.

Edwin was a few steps ahead of her clearing the way. He was holding her hand when he let go. Suddenly, he bent over and grabbed the streetlight pole. He undid his gun holster. The gun was raised to shoot at someone. Gloria couldn't see anyone running.

The bullet hit the streetlight a hundred yards away as Edwin lurched forward. The shattered glass rained down on the hanging flowerpot which shielded the man underneath. The clown briefly slowed, wiped off the glass, and then disappeared around a corner.

Gloria saw the back of the clown's head. She knew the clown under the flowerpot was taking back alleys to reach the subway.

She went over to Edwin and saw the knife stuck above his shirt pocket. Immediately Gloria dialed the emergency number.

"Edwin, talk to me."

He leaned on her.

"There was a clown with a knife. I never saw the knife until it was too late. Sorry I missed him with my gun."

A police officer ran over to see what was wrong. He called a police van which arrived within minutes. The van was previously monitoring the parade route. Several police officers went in the direction Gloria pointed to look for the street attacker.

Gloria gave him her sweater to staunch the blood. Edwin sat in the police van until the emergency vehicle arrived. They took him to the nearest hospital.

The police took Gloria to the hospital emergency room to wait. The doctors rushed her bodyguard into surgery. Gloria called Rory and Stan. Stan picked up Edwin's wife and drove her to the hospital.

The group waited for the doctor. Finally, the doctor came out with a small cardboard box. The box was ripped open and bloody. He took the tiny earring plastic packet out and gave the earrings to Edwin's wife.

"The police will want the box and card for evidence, but Edwin told me the earrings were for his daughter. The man is going to be fine. We need to keep him until tomorrow. The surgery was quick, and the wound should heal nicely. He'll need a few days off. His wife can visit with him after he comes out of recovery."

Gloria let the police know about her clown wig package. An officer followed Gloria and Rory home. The paper packaging and clown wig were taken for evidence.

After the police officer left, Rory was upset Gloria didn't tell him about receiving the wig.

"Anything strange that happens, we will discuss whatever it is together, right, Gloria."

"You needed a break. I thought the package was misdelivered. I made a bad decision."

Rory remembered telling her no more speculation.

"I didn't know the wig was a message to scare me. The knife person hurt my bodyguard to show me how easy a target that I am. But then maybe it was from the weird neighbor that Edwin kicked in the butt."

Frazzled by the ordeal, Rory took his wife into his arms. He looked into her eyes.

"Gloria, talk to me even if I tell you not to bother me. This attack is a wake-up call. None of us is immune from danger. From now on, you always carry a gun. If anyone steps in front of you, shoot."

"Maybe we are overreacting," said Gloria.

"No. This person is real, and there's only one way to stop the psycho dead in their tracks. Shoot to kill. This time choose the head or heart. I don't care which one."

Gloria thought about her husband's speech.

"I'll shoot the head."

"Good."

They talked with Stan who was at the hospital. Edwin was doing better. Rory contacted the Security people in their building about the delivery person. All their security could tell them was the kid showed them his plastic paper badge, and they let him in the building.

Rory called the delivery company, and the person's name wasn't on their list of employees. He recommended they get better badges because their current ones were too easy to copy.

Rory stayed and worked from home until Edwin could guard his wife. Rory didn't trust anybody to protect his wife other than Edwin. He knew their bodyguard would now be stronger in his vigilance.

Edwin Sherman would want revenge just like Rory did.

39 Dan's Revelation

Dan Gibbons removed his ballet shoes when Gloria walked into the men's locker room to see him. Her bodyguard held the door open.

"Gloria, this is not a good place for you to visit me. This is the men's room. There are disgusting urinals."

"We counted the number of men that went in and out the door. The urinals don't look too bad."

Dan shook his head. Gloria was unpredictable.

"Still, let's go outside. You never know who might have snuck in when you weren't looking. I thought I was alone once, and a female janitor was wearing a bright pink outfit. The outfit didn't go well with her red and purple hair. I didn't know people could buy those colors. It was her face tattoo that scared me more plus her cleaning gear for the stalls. The knife tattoo bent when she frowned. Then she pointed her bleach spray bottle at me. The plastic bottle showed a skull head for poison. Where do the commercial people buy that stuff?" I've never run so fast out of a men's room in my life. Besides, these dance costumes are expensive to replace if they get ruined by a crazy person."

Edwin grinned about the scenario. He followed them outside and watched the area. He couldn't see any clowns, pink ladies, or weapons. He relaxed and lit a cigarette.

"Why are you paying me a visit, Gloria?"

"I need to talk to you about Bella. Her distant cousin told me that Bella was having an affair with a dancer from our troupe since Atlantic City. I couldn't believe the story. Bella didn't seem the type to cheat. Do you know which dancer she was seeing?"

Dan did know. He hesitated.

"Well?"

"Sure, I saw them together backstage. It was uncanny to keep running into them. After a while, they were embarrassed. They met later because I never saw them alone with each other again. They were more cautious. The man was Dillon."

Gloria's face registered partial shock.

"You knew and didn't tell me?"

Dan wasn't sure why she was so upset.

"I thought maybe Dillon would have told you. The two of you were tight."

Gloria looked at Dan skeptically.

"Hey, I can read the signs just like anybody else."

"Well, Dillon didn't talk about Bella, and he hasn't even told the police about the affair."

Dan wasn't surprised.

"Dillon wouldn't talk about any of his affairs, nor would he hurt a woman. He loved them too much. He was after you in Atlantic City and turned to Bella. She fell for his monotonous crap. His silence is the best way for him to stay out of the investigation. Dillon would save himself."

She was right where Rory stopped her the previous evening. She was stuck in her investigation other than knowing more about Bella's affair. There wasn't a way to contact Dillon.

"The cousin told me that Clark wasn't doing too well. Bella's husband was fired from his job due to numerous sick days which the dancing company felt were beyond reasonable. He's not dancing with any other company. She told me he was on unemployment, and the money now has stopped."

Dan looked at Gloria and shook his head. They hated to see someone give up dancing.

"Who else knew about the two dancers?" asked Gloria.

Dan thought about the other people on the troupe and the ballet outsiders.

"That's sad news about Clark. Some people take longer to mourn a loss. I assume he's mourning. Johnny knew about the affair. I made the mistake of telling him. I don't believe Bella's husband knew about Dillon."

Gloria watched her bodyguard walk toward them.

"Johnny Zander is a user and a little creep. With Clark out of money, Zander can't get rich off Clark. I wonder what he's done with the affair information. I'm sure he is planning to use the story. A love affair would make another book. He might be planning to get all the dirt first by using the players. People love to read about disastrous reactions. The way Zander embellished the book about me would make his next book simple to write."

Dan grew serious.

"Wow. My head is spinning the wheels. Johnny would want to create massive tension by riling people's insides. He gravitates toward a mess. My ex-boyfriend would try to sell the secret. He would find other buyers. I'm not sure who would want to buy a dancer's story. I'll have to think about where he would go. Johnny does like money and gifts, especially now. My comfortable funds are out of the picture. All he and Clark have left are probably their credit cards."

"You mean that he might try to sell the story to someone like the news media. I don't think the news would care about an affair now that Bella is dead."

Dan took off his suspenders and folded them on his lap.

"Johnny called me the other day. He told me to meet him at the checkout counter in the men's department because he wanted to buy me a new suit. There was a hint in his voice about a windfall. He told me about a reporter friend that he knew. I didn't catch the name, but I can call him back. We didn't meet. I don't need a suit."

Edwin pointed at his watch. They needed to leave.

"Talk with him and call me with the reporter's name."

Dan went inside to change clothes. Edwin and Gloria left.

Gloria was driving when Edwin said, "I checked the other day. The reporter at your old apartment is out on bail. We might want to ask him a few questions. He's the type of reporter that would sell sleazy news or run around with the same type of men like Zander."

"He's also the type of person who might know about clowns."

Edwin rubbed his shoulder.

"I'll try to find the reporter man without you. I will bring my reinforcements just in case he decides to not open his mouth. We shouldn't tell Rory what we are up to. He was upset about the peeping-tom incident. Maybe we can let him know later."

Gloria knew keeping Rory out of the loop would backfire on her.

"I don't know. He was mad about your getting knifed and my not telling him about a clown wig package. He wants me to communicate better."

Edwin agreed to run their news past Rory.

Rory sat at his desk in the studio building. He was not amused by the information from Edwin.

"Gloria stays out of this little game. You can try talking with Zander and the news reporter. I don't think you will get far with either one of the men."

His cell phone rang.

"Sweetheart, how's your dad? Good, we were just talking about you. The answer is an emphatic, *No*."

Gloria hated to follow his advice. She spoke. "Dan told me Zander is out of the country so he couldn't get the reporter's name. You will never guess where he went?"

Rory sat up in his chair. "No!"

"Yes, he is on an airplane to Vienna."

They both knew what minor problem Dillon might be dealing with on his own.

"You think Zander will threaten Dillon with exposure. Dillon makes good money."

"Now can I be in the game?"

Edwin watched Rory's hard-faced expression.

"No. I mean it, Gloria."

Rory disconnected the call from his wife.

"She is out. If she continues with her part in this strange pursuit, I will fire you on the spot."

Edwin looked in the air and stood up to leave.

"I'll go home and tell my wife you fired me today. You know Gloria isn't going to stop. She's persistently brave, and that's why we like her."

Edwin hesitated at the door.

"All right. You can keep this job. We still let Gloria believe my answer stands. Is that understood? I want her to think before she leaps."

"Yes. I'll ask my contact about the newspaperman. We'll wait until Zander returns. I don't speak any foreign languages. Also, I got lost at London airport once. I forgot what level and gate my next flight was on after losing my ticket in the men's room."

"You could have checked with the airline."

"I did but missed my connection and had to rebook a flight for the next day. I couldn't believe how expensive first-class cost. The standby seats were already taken."

"We'll wait for Zander," suggested Rory.

40 Zander's Bad Moves

Before Johnny Zander flew to Vienna, he contacted Clark to see if he could pony up any money to buy a story about his dead wife, Bella. Zander believed the man might have money from a life insurance policy. Of course, Clark did not have money, but he still showed funds available on his credit cards.

Zander didn't care where the money came from for the story. A person could withdraw some cash from credit cards as a down payment. From there, the person would be put on a monthly payment plan.

Mistakenly, Zander told Clark where he was traveling and the hotel name where he was going to stay for a week. He trusted that Clark might change his mind about buying the story.

Johnny also told a reporter about the existence of a story. The reporter named Randy wanted the story for free. Zander was a bright bulb and pressured the man. He also gave him the name of the hotel in Vienna in case the reporter found the funds.

Upon reaching Vienna, Zander was not aware that he was being followed. He met with Dillon and received a packet of blackmail cash. The dancer looked around worried there might be police officers.

"You promise this story about my affair with Bella will not be sold to anyone else?"

Johnny lied.

The two men separated. Johnny went back to his hotel and ordered room service. Thinking the knock was his food for the evening, Zander opened the door.

The food tray would be left outside Zander's room. When the house cleaner entered the hotel room, she would see the cracked mirror, broken chair, and blood on the bed cover.

She immediately called hotel security who found Zander hanging from the shower with his shaver cord. He was dead. The police determined the man was murdered.

They caught an American reporter on the hotel video in the bar talking with Zander. Randy Ruffin was immediately arrested.

XXXXXX

Dillon was glad to have given Johnny the money. Now he could move on with his dancing career and not worry. He decided to go swimming at the beach. The beach was his usual weekend spot. The place was good for picking up lonely women.

There was one area with some steps that he liked to use. The water was deep and a good place to dive. There was a small metal dock next to the steps. He would swim laps and then return underwater to the dock.

He swam a few laps and stopped because he heard a boat in the vicinity. The boat kept getting closer and closer. Dillon saw the driver and dove under the water before the fiberglass ran over him.

He surfaced and saw the boat was returning. Dillon realized what happened. He was in deep trouble.

The man in the boat meant to kill him. He started swimming to shore and dove again.

The large boat roared past him.

Two teenage boys saw the nut job in the boat run over the man in the water twice. They went running in their swim trunks and sandals to find the police. One of the boys tripped over his towel and saw the boat searching the water and then leave extremely fast. They ran.

Gloria was at home watching the news. Rory entered their condominium.

"Hush! The announcer is talking about some strange events that happened in Vienna."

They listened to the announcer and were stunned by the recent events. Gloria couldn't believe the announcer.

"Dillon is missing. He never showed for his ballet performance. He would never miss his dance routines for any reason. Dancing is his life."

"Well, maybe whatever he was working on didn't pan out. There's a perfectly good reason for his disappearance. I'm sure Dillon will present himself eventually. Maybe another opportunity was better than his current one."

"You think he's still alive?" asked Gloria.

"Does our cat have more than nine lives? He leaps from the floor to the top of the refrigerator to reach the French bread in the large basket you've stashed there. He doesn't eat the bread but likes to chew on the plastic."

Gloria argued with him.

"She likes the top of the refrigerator. The basket is the draw now that I've placed a comfortable towel inside. The reason she chooses this spot is not the bread or the bag."

"Whatever. Anyway, Dillon has cat survivor instincts. We're talking two cats or eighteen lives. A lot of men would have punched him out by now. I certainly thought about it, but there were too many people around."

Gloria remembered an opening night.

"You're the one with the personal grudge because of a movie. The movie meant nothing to me except for the money. He is human, and humans do die."

Rory disagreed. Dillon gone from the earth wouldn't be a terrible thing for him. There was his wife who did care no matter what she said.

"Look, you have to remember he's strong and a smooth talker. I've seen the man leap high and land without so much as a sound. He and Mara would make a great pair. The smooth talker part is how he can slide in and out of women and countries. He's probably gone to Africa for a holiday or some odd place equally unappealing to normal people."

Gloria frowned. Dillon would like to live in Africa.

"I feel there's more unwelcome news coming. My hand itches like there's a storm brewing."

Rory saw the news earlier.

"You have beginning arthritis from bending your hands so much while dancing. Rain shouldn't be

213

a problem. The weather here is supposed to be sunny all day."

Rory was trying to distract her. Gloria went out to the patio. She felt several drops of rain. Her husband put the leash on the cat and joined her with two cups of coffee.

She accepted her cup. The cell phone in her pocket vibrated. Placing the cup down on the table, she saw the call was from Dan.

Dan's voice sounded strange.

"They found Johnny in his hotel room in Vienna. The police say they think that he was murdered. His sister called me an hour ago."

Gloria put the phone on speaker.

"We're sorry, Dan, about your friend, Zander. How did he die?"

Dan cringed.

"Zander was no longer my friend. He was hanged in the bathroom. Don't worry, I'm all right. We separated a long time ago. I won't be going to his funeral. Before he left, I did tell Johnny not to go alone. He never listened to me before. Why would he listen to me now? Something bad did happen. Oh, there's more to the story. The police have arrested this stranger from America. I've never met him, nor do I get their connection. The police have a video of the two men meeting. The man wasn't Johnny's type. There's another mystery. The police found a clown wig and costume in the newspaperman's suitcase. Zander wouldn't date a clown or sell a story to one. Anyway, he would have to be desperate to do so. He didn't like clowns much like Dillon. Zander was more into zoo monkeys. Hard to believe, I know."

Gloria asked for the arrested man's name. Dan told them.

Rory and Gloria were speechless.

Dan thought he was cut off. He looked at his cell phone.

"Are the two of you still there? Hello?"

Rory spoke.

"The reporter that the Vienna police arrested was probably the clown who attacked Edwin Sherman, our bodyguard. Randy Ruffin was also the peeping tom that watched Gloria when we lived at our old apartment. He was arrested for that little item but recently got out of prison. We've been trying to find him. I'll contact the police here about Randy, so they check the description of the clown suit. They can connect him to the crime in America. Now we wonder if Zander told Clark about Bella and Dillon. Maybe that's why Dillon is missing?"

After explaining the news regarding Dillon, they hung up the phone and went back inside.

"Gloria, you were right. I can't believe we are having a downpour and some hail."

"I told you a storm was brewing."

Rory looked at his wife.

"You're spooky."

She took the French bread off the refrigerator and placed the bag on the counter. The cat sniffed at the bread, jumped on top of the refrigerator, and laid down.

"As I said, you are one super spooky woman. Remind me to stay on your good side."

She took the large knife out of the drawer and sliced the bread.

Rory threw up his hands.

"Maybe we should get a dartboard for you to take out your frustrations."

Gloria handed him a piece of buttered cinnamon raisin bread and snatched it back.

"Come here. I love my spooky woman who is talented and beautiful. You are the best."

Gloria stared at him.

"Pretty please."

The cat beat her into his open arms. Gloria ate the buttered bread but made a second one for her husband.

41 Electronic Gadgets

Edwin left Gloria with Rory at his work studio. The middle of the room was filled with empty boxes. There were electricians installing pipes and new wiring for some electronic equipment he ordered.

Rory was like a kid with a new box of toys. The carpenter hammered the display box to the wall. She saw him placing her awards behind the glass cases.

"Thank you. They look better here than in our old apartment. The display is impressive."

"The display isn't the reason I called. I see you received my message and have your leotards on. The men should be done in fifteen minutes, and we can test the new system out. I've taken one of your first videos and loaded the video to the new software. Let's go to the viewing room. Then we can try a dance afterward."

"Which dance would you like me to select?"

"You choose one."

Gloria was working on contemporary dance. This dance was different. Rory hadn't seen the moves.

"Okay, I have a new one in mind."

Rory's eyebrows raised.

"I squeezed the routine in between my ballet workouts. That's why I've been an hour late for over a month. The dance is a birthday surprise."

In the viewing room, she watched her old video. He turned the lights on.

"Like this software changes everything in the dance video."

Rory watched as her eyes lit up. He liked the way she looked. They went out to the open studio.

The boxes were removed from the floor, and the workers swept any loose packing from the studio. He took the tiny remote and showed her the buttons to start, stop, the music buttons, and the lights.

"What do I do with the remote after the first button?"

"The remote is in a protective case. You will have five seconds before the music starts. I've put a mat over to the right side for now. Throw the remote in the direction you begin your routine. I've watched, and they usually start on the right side."

"Gloria, it's 1, 2, 3, and 4."

"Exactly."

He clipped the tiny microphone onto her top. She knew the rest of the buttons. She only needed to speak softly. The microphone would trigger the rest of the system.

"Why do I need a separate remote, and why are there empty buttons?"

The remote will start the video rolling and the music you've selected from our sound system box on the wall. You must select the song beforehand. The empty buttons are for future lights."

They experimented with the remote. Rory showed her how to erase and go back to the beginning. He explained they would work on the more sophisticated additional lights later.

"Let's see you dance."

218

Gloria positioned herself, clicked the remote start, threw the remote, and counted.

She was in the dark and several revolving spotlights lit her body. Gloria began her dance routine. Rory watched fascinated as she talked in the microphone. He could hear her commands in his headset. They were recording her voice in time to the video recorder.

He stopped looking at his control screen on the computer. Rory watched his wife dance. This dance was different. He smiled and relaxed in his chair. Her ballet dancing experience added to the extra steps.

She stopped dancing to full lights and bowed. Gloria counted and went over to the remote to turn off the music and video. Rory could have stopped them on his computer. Wanting her to have the ability to dance without a director was important.

He watched her drink the chilly water.

"Great job!"

She was disappointed.

Rory picked up his wife and swung her around.

"You were heaven wrapped in a pretty package. If I was a deck of cards standing on end, you blew them away. I went crazy just watching you."

"Too much."

"Never."

They went into the viewing room and watched the video. Rory and Gloria were happy. He would tweak the video, and they would send the item to their lawyer for copyright. The video would be her next resume for promoting her dance studio.

"We bought the building next door this morning."

Gloria squealed with delight. The architect's plans were being drawn.

"Are you happy now?"

"I'm pleased beyond normal. I'm ecstatic to have my place. You will be right next door most of the time."

42 The Box at the Inn

Guy Strand sat with Gloria at a table at his place. Stan brought over a glass of orange juice and milk to their table. He left to train a new person as a server.

"Why does my daughter have a sad face today?"

She sat up straight and stretched her legs.

"I'm stuck in finding Bella's killer. The police aren't moving fast to find the person. I don't think they have any suspects."

"Well, there are some facts and assumptions we know that might help. Zander went to Vienna. Assumption 1: We believe he went there to get money from Dillon. Dan told you Zander talked about getting a windfall soon, and Dillon was the only person he knew there."

Gloria continued, "Zander tangled with a robber and was murdered. Assumption 2: We believe Dillon gave Zander money to keep his mouth shut about his affair with Bella. Someone found out about the money."

Guy drank his orange juice.

"This is where you are stuck in your story. Let's say Zander blabbed to more than just Dan. Who knew Zander had the money? Dillon wouldn't kill the man because he would get arrested. His dancing was more important. Next, we find Dillon is missing. Why kill Zander and run over Dillon with a boat? Are we sure this newspaper guy killed Zander or tried to run over Dillon? The newspaper guy was a chump and was in the wrong place. He was the clown though who knifed Edwin. Therefore, we have a stranger who killed Zander and rented a boat in Vienna. Did Zander ever meet Clark?"

"I don't recall the two men being in the same room. I wonder. My questions and answers match some of your thinking. You believe the stranger person is the same, plus the killer of Bella."

Her father swirled his glass. He chewed on an ice cube.

"There was this old black and white film called *The Box at the Inn*. The story was about a writer who went to stay at an Inn. She was stuck with her book writing."

She vaguely remembered. "When the writer arrives, she walks through the place. There's no one in the rooms."

Guy intervened.

"The Inn appears to be empty."

Gloria knew where the people might have gone. Her father continued.

"Cautiously, she approaches the last room, and inside there is a large cardboard box. Frightened by a sound, she climbs inside the box and finds a black feather and a loaded gun. The lid automatically shuts on the box."

Gloria noticed the analogy.

"I'm inside the box. Somehow, I didn't close the box. Who closed the box? There might be a reason. The room is protecting the woman. Only this time, while inside the box where it's presumed to be a safety

222

zone, she finds there are two clues. The feather somehow drops silently into the box. The gun represents the object hidden by someone."

Her father scratched his head.

"You are almost correct. In the film, a person enters the last room and sees the box. The writer remains hidden and is incredibly quiet. She has a choice. She can reveal herself or not. In her mind, she decides to stay hidden until she has more information."

Gloria thought about the plot.

"The stranger tries to open the box. He can't until the woman chooses to reveal herself or someone in the room whispers. Who in the world would give her away?"

"See how much more difficult things have become," said Guy.

Gloria tried to figure out the puzzle. She continued.

"The man again tries to open the box and is successful. He sees the two clues and the woman. This person is holding a knife. She has a gun and changes her mind when she sees the man's hat. The hat carries the same black feather. Realizing the feather in the box belongs to the man, she picks up the gun. She unclicks the safety switch. He is the reason the Inn is empty of its occupants."

Her father encouragingly said, "Now, Gloria, keep going."

"The woman is in danger because she has figured out the clues. The killer knows that she knows. She caresses the blue steel of the gun. The walls reflect the victims' shadows when the sun hits the room. He hid the bodies in the wall. No one should have died. They were nice people living their life and having a vacation."

"Now it is up to her to make a decision. The man never gave the victims a choice. He won't give her a choice either."

Gloria understood about choices.

"Right or wrong. There is only one way out. She shoots the killer dead. Stepping out of the box, the woman freely walks away from the Inn and finishes her book."

"Very good."

Stan came over to their table.

"What did I miss?"

Both Gloria and Guy talked at once, "*The Box at the Inn.*"

Stan smacked his forehead.

"That movie scared the crap out of me, and I watch all kinds of movies. Oh, I've got to show the new guy where we keep the trash."

"No problem, we can handle things."

Guy finished his juice.

"When bad people find money, the first thing they do is buy something big. There's one clue. However, there might have been something else worth stealing in the room. If the killer stole the second item, you might find the other clue."

"So, I need to find two clues to solve my case."

Edwin walked into the bistro and told her that his car was repaired. They could go to the gym.

"What two clues?" asked Edwin.

Both Gloria and Guy talked at once, "*The Box at the Inn.*"

Edwin felt for his pack of cigarettes and stopped.

"Oh, no, don't climb in the box. If you do, you'll be in big trouble. I wouldn't even go to that crazy Inn. Where was that place? If I remember the Inn was close to Beaufort. After I saw that movie, I went home and threw all those extra moving boxes in my garage in the dumpster. I told my wife we were never going on vacation to Beaufort. We might accidentally be killed by the nerd."

Gloria thought about her father's last sentence. She knew the answer wasn't a gun.

"I'm looking for a feather falling into my lap."

Edwin sat down in the extra chair.

"Great. While you're looking for the feather, the bird shit will fall and hit me smack dab in the head."

Gloria and her father broke out laughing. She stood up to leave. Edwin joined her.

"Goodbye, dad."

"Good luck, Gloria. Stay safe."

Edwin was quiet on the way home. Gloria was someone who wasn't afraid of the dark. Edwin respected the dark. There was a difference between the two of them. He knew better not to stir the pot unless necessary.

He dropped Gloria off at her door.

Edwin stepped into his car. Turning the key, he realized how important his client was to him on a personal level. When the time came, he would have to climb in the box with her. Their combined force would help.

"Two large guns are always better than one. The impact will shatter more than glass. Feathers. Who needs lightweight feathers?"

Edwin was rattled by the movie concept.

"Maybe I should look at those trucks that look like Sherman tanks. Hey, everybody, here comes Sherman in his Sherman. Get the heck out of the way! Clear the streets. Heavy Sherman is coming through."

Edwin drove to his home and stopped at the bakery on the way.

He heard they were making chocolate eclairs. His daughter was crazy about the vanilla filling. She didn't care for the strawberry ones.

Edwin was left to eat the chocolate top which was the best part. He ordered an extra eclair and took a bite.

"My daughter is correct; the pudding is good."

He finished eating his éclair and felt better.

"I hate boxes and salespeople who won't sell me a fishing net. I should call my buddy at that store."

43 Third Dancer

Her shoes were worn on the toes. The stuffing was showing through. Gloria would need to dig out a new pair of ballet shoes from her closet at home. The third dancer from her ballet company sat down on the long bench and began untying her shoes.

"Hi, Tanya, the practice session was good today."

Tanya Adams looked at Gloria. "You sound like you have a cold."

Gloria covered her mouth and sneezed into a kerchief.

"I've been tired and my legs ache. We've been pushing things pretty hard."

"I know. The reason I wanted to talk to you is personal. A rumor has been going around that your husband is building you a novel dance studio. Would you let me know when you plan to leave? I want to apply for the second dancer position."

"Sure, I don't have a date yet. When I have a better grip on my plans, we'll talk. I can even recommend you for the position."

Tanya hugged Gloria and quickly pulled away for fear of catching her cold.

"That would be so wonderful. Clark wanted me to ask you for a reference, and you volunteered."

Gloria looked blankly at Tanya. She blinked in surprise.

"You've been dating someone named Clark. Do I know this person?"

Tanya put her jeans on and pulled on a sweatshirt.

"His name is Clark Reine. He has this cool British sports car, and we go for drives in the country. He used to be a dancer but teaches language classes part-time now at a small college. The man still lifts weights to stay in shape."

Gloria was stunned by her comments.

"Doesn't that type of sports car cost a lot of coins? The car can be very pricey for a teacher's salary when all the options are chosen?"

"The car has extras. I don't know the price of the car. He might have paid cash or gotten a loan for the vehicle. He never said. I understand you do know him from the Columbia Dance Troupe. Clark mentioned that his former wife liked you very much. She was at your wedding. He told me some of the cities the troupe traveled, and the pranks left in the hotel rooms."

Gloria put her ballet shoes away and put on her zippered sweatshirt. She took the lip gloss and touched her chapped lips. A lemon cough drop was put in her mouth.

"Bella and I were good friends. We met outside in New York City when I saw the advertisement for dancers. It seems long ago. She encouraged me to apply. I miss talking with her about various ballet movements. She gave me the name of some good costume designers. She glowed at my wedding and seemed happy. I'm surprised Clark talked about her. I thought he was despondent and lost his job a while back. I knew he spoke French, but I find it odd he stopped dancing."

Tanya nodded.

"Bella's death was such a tragedy. He doesn't like to talk about her. I know he quit the dance floor scene. One night, he came to the ballet, and we ran into each other at an after-party. He missed being around the dancers. We are an odd breed of cats. We work hard to perform a series of shows. Then we have to relearn a new show."

Gloria was not sure how she felt about the information regarding Clark. Caution flags waved in her head. Tanya kept talking.

"Clark has moved on and doesn't miss the demanding work. He likes his new job, and we are having an enjoyable time. However, he's been pressuring me to get married. I want to make the second position dancer before I take the plunge. Career first is my motto."

Gloria completely understood. She smiled remembering how difficult the decision to marry was for her. The timing was the issue.

"Besides, I think we haven't known each other long enough. I used to think I would marry a man who had a forty-acre ranch in the country with purebred horses. Dream on with the horse thing. Well, I must run. My mom is in town visiting me. Clark went nuts when I told him that I was busy this weekend. Men want all the attention."

Gloria watched Tanya leave the women's locker room. Her brain was riveting back and forth.

"I have a massive headache. That won't be good. We have six performances scheduled."

She went outside and met Edwin. He saw how pale Gloria looked. They went to a small café, and she ordered the chicken noodle soup. Her throat was feeling scratchy. Her head throbbed.

Gloria forgot to mention her discussion with Tanya to Edwin and Rory.

By the time she arrived home, her fever was hotter. The thermometer showed a high fever. Rory took her to the emergency room. She was put in the hospital with pneumonia.

Gloria canceled out three of the ballet performances. An alternate female dancer took her place.

Flowers arrived and were brought into her hospital room. The nurse showed her the card. The red roses and yellow lilies were from Clark Reine. Gloria let the nurse take the flowers to the front desk or deliver them to any other patient.

She didn't want those flowers in her room. Those two flowers were her friend, Geri's favorite combination. She tried to think back to when they were in the dance troupe.

"How did Clark know about the flowers? He wasn't at the funeral to see her photograph. The Reine's have never been inside Geri's parent's house. Bella told her husband. But then, how would Bella know about the flowers? The troupe company kept our photos in our personnel files. I didn't talk with Clark since

Bella's or Geri's death. Very strange to have picked the combination."

Gloria would ask Rory's assistant to send the thank you notes. Her doctor walked in with the good news. She could be released after lunch.

She was glad to get out of the hospital. Her flowers were given to other patients. She kept the cards except for one. Then she changed her mind and added the card to the pile.

"There was no reason to irritate the man."

She was home recuperating when she mentioned Tanya to Edwin.

"You mean a dancer at your ballet company is dating Clark. This guy is the one with the murdered wife who also was a dancer that you knew?"

"Yes."

"I'm feeling the heebie-jeebies. I would think the man would stay far away from the dance arena. The police haven't found his wife's killer. Then you tell me he sent you the type of flowers that your dead friend, Geri, liked. This is unreal."

Gloria looked at her hot tea and saw the leaves in her cup.

"I knew a lady who could read these tea leaves. She died from old age. Her daughter said she was over a hundred years old. I wonder what she would tell me if she were here. Her daughter might have the same skills."

"No way, give me that cup."

She handed Edwin her cup.

He responded.

"Hello, is anybody there? Come out, come out wherever you are. We want you to tell us whether my favorite football team is going to win this year. If football is not in your database, how about baseball?"

He handed her back the cup.

"There's nobody home."

"Very funny. Come out, come out is a child's game."

Gloria threw her blanket aside and went to refill her cup.

"Try putting a little lemon into your drink this time. I see fruits all the time on the television talking to each other. They usually are trying to sell underwear. But my wife tells me lemons help a sore throat."

"Edwin be serious. I'm thinking about the film my father mentioned. Maybe the writer should have sat with a cup of tea in her box and asked the dead lady in the wall to read the leaves."

"Oh, boy! You are nuttier than a fruitcake today. You make fun of me using a child's game. The game on this table is much more difficult to play. You are wondering where Clark found the money to buy his fancy car. You know banks do hand out cash for a loan. I didn't need any tea leaves to figure out how financial institutions work."

She stirred in some lemon from a plastic bottle.

"You aren't using real lemons? Real ones are better."

"I'll get some lemons from my neighbors. I know banks will give you cash. I thought Tanya's comments were strange. Maybe it was her use of the word nuts to describe how Clark felt about her mom visiting."

Edwin shook his head. He just called Gloria nuts earlier.

"Men talk that way about potential mothers-in-law. Their response is an automatic and super-fast gut reaction."

"Oh, men! You and Rory think alike. I can see this conversation is going nowhere. I'll get dressed and you can take me to my doctor's appointment. I need his authorization before I can return to ballet practice."

They went downtown, and she did receive the slip from her doctor. Edwin bought her some real lemons at the market across the street.

Gloria went back to rehearsals and completed the last three performances with the ballet company. She could take a break for a couple of months. She wouldn't see Tanya for some time.

The brick walls of Gloria's dance studio were done, and the new roof was completed. A new building replaced the old one. When she and Edwin stopped by the building, the contractors were installing the new windows and doors.

She went into Rory's office to let him know they made a good decision to put the parking underground on two floors. There would be a guard at the entrance to the garage.

He took her on a tour of the almost-finished building. There were samples of the flooring and paint for her to select. They quickly decided the colors and looked at the drapes. Gloria selected a pale grey that would allow some light to enter. The bathroom fixtures were chosen and the dance lockers.

Gloria was glad to be done with the design process. Now she could work on the dance class outlines. Rory let her use the office computer. When they were done, they went home.

She told him about Tanya and Clark. He was surprised as she was about the budding relationship. Rory didn't think the purchase of a sports car was unusual or any cause for alarm.

"Rory, the police didn't investigate Bella's murder. The first suspect is always the husband. They glossed over this murder because the police were busy with the drug bust, we read about in the newspaper."

"You need to stop obsessing about the Bella murder case. They will catch the horrible person. Murder investigations take time."

She decided to call someone sympathetic like her father.

He asked Gloria how well she knew the man. Gloria had to admit there wasn't a whole lot. Most of her conversations were with Bella talking girl-talk. She approached Dan.

Dan listened to recent events. He knew Tanya from some of the parties they both attended. He told her about an incident where Bella missed a step and tripped Clark while they were at practice with the troupe.

"I know it was when we were in Atlanta. There was some strain happening between the two dancers which you and I later figured out."

"You are saying Clark displayed a nasty temper?"

Dan shook his head.

"Positive. Bella snapped back at Clark. The man threw her shoes at the wall and stomped out of the building. I drove Bella home after Clark left her stranded at practice."

Gloria wondered about the slip in personality. The two dancers never showed their anger while they were performing. She would have noticed.

"The distance was in the air, or I was too busy with Rory. Being in love makes the world seem rosy. I missed the strain in their marriage."

Gloria stopped in the theatre room and waited for Edwin. Suddenly, she remembered Bella looking flushed.

"Bella was having an affair in Atlanta and possibly earlier. There might have been others who weren't dancers. A dancer could have made the situation more explosive. She most certainly wasn't in love with her husband."

44 The Feather

Tanya went to the mall for some early morning shopping. The department store was open for fifteen minutes and was almost empty. She saw Gloria walk by the perfume counter. She dropped her necklace on the glass case and told the fine jewelry woman that she would be back.

"Gloria, this is truly funny. We don't see each other for months, and we choose the same store. I'm glad we ran into each other. There's a necklace that I want you to see. I've been here twice looking at the design. Today is decision day."

Gloria glanced at the jewelry counter.

"I'm out looking for some cologne before I head to the evening dresses. I want to get a dress that is elegant and simple for my dance studio's grand opening."

"Oh, then you've turned in your notice to the ballet company?"

"Not yet. I thought I would wait until our grand opening is over. We have hired some dance instructors to do some introductory classes. Rory wants to see how the students' skill levels compare before we do the more advanced classes which I will teach."

Tanya was thrilled for her newfound friend. She told her something in confidence.

"I'm exchanging a necklace that Clark gave me. The design isn't quite my style. The sales clerk is having a tough time finding the necklace in their

236

catalog. Come with me to the jewelry counter where we can talk some more."

The two women proceeded to the fine jewelry counter. They could see the sales clerk with her manager pouring over a large book. They moved on to a second book and were turning pages.

"Clark doesn't understand my taste very well. I hate thick gold necklaces. They remind me of those huge muscle wrestlers. He seemed mad at me for not liking the piece of jewelry. Clark doesn't know I'm going to exchange the piece. I have talked with my mom, and she told me that I should move on and find a man who isn't so controlling."

Gloria sympathized with Tanya. Tanya took their trust in each other a step further. She confided to Gloria.

"We are friends. I need to talk to someone."

"I'm here whenever you need me," offered Gloria.

Tanya hesitated and then blurted out her plan.

"I haven't told Clark yet, but I'm going to break off our relationship once we start ballet practice and rehearsals."

"You've only dated for four months. I'm sorry things aren't working."

"After two months, he stopped being nice, if you know what I mean."

Gloria could guess.

"I should be going to the top floor. I see Edwin getting impatient. He's dropped the cologne bottle twice. There are always more men waiting in the wings. You should trust your instincts."

They watched the jewelry department manager come to where they were standing. The manager handed the necklace back to Tanya. Gloria saw the necklace and frowned.

"Let me see the design."

Tanya showed her the necklace.

"How strange? Dan bought his friend, Johnny, a necklace that looks like this one. I remember the design and have a photo of the two of them. He bought the necklace at Maxine Stein's store. He told me the necklace cost over four thousand dollars."

The manager shook her head. "We don't carry this particular design from the Larkin Company. Therefore, we can't do an exchange for your necklace. You might try Stein's store."

Tanya was excited about the price she might receive for the heavy necklace. Gloria told Tanya to let her know if Stein's store would exchange her necklace for a comparable one.

Edwin followed Gloria to the expensive dresses and waited outside the dressing room in a chair. Finding a red dress with black trim on the top, they made their exit to the car in the parking ramp.

Gloria's cell phone rang. It was Tanya letting her know Stein's store allowed the exchange. She purchased a slimmer chain of a higher quality gold count and matching earrings. She texted a photograph to Gloria of the new necklace alongside the old one.

Edwin drove Gloria home.

Getting on her husband's computer, she enlarged a photograph of the Atlantic City dance troupe tour. She saw Johnny Zander's necklace. She looked at the uploaded photograph from Tanya. The necklace was the same design.

Gloria went to Stein's website and found they owned a store near the casino in Atlantic City. They verified the heavy gold necklace she found on their website was sold the same weekend at the Atlantic City store.

The weekend was the same timeframe the dance troupe was in town. They couldn't give her the name of the client.

She pushed back from the computer and closed the screens.

"I think that I've found the feather. Now, what do I do with the information? Sit in the box and hope he doesn't notice or do I get the police involved?"

The decision was currently hers to make. She decided to wait until after her new studio's grand opening party. Her opening a studio was important. This was her dream.

"Clark could have purchased the necklace in New York City. I might be wanting a match, so there would be a clue to match my wish. In my haste, the disclosure could alert the true killer to my intentions. Those intentions are to find Bella's killer. She and her family must have justice. Or is this a bad idea?"

Gloria heard the lock turning. Rory was home with a take-out dinner. She shut the computer off and went to greet her husband.

239

His eyes lit up when she showed him the strapless dress and new heels.

"Your dress is very pretty. I'm glad you found what you were looking for this morning. Anything else unusual happening today?"

"I did run into Tanya. She was exchanging a necklace. She wanted to know if we had chosen a date to terminate my job with the ballet company."

Rory checked his calendar.

"I think we can be safe in turning in your notice in a month."

Gloria smiled.

"I have loved my work at the ballet company, but I am looking forward to acting as the boss. Besides, my commute will be shorter and more pleasurable with you close."

Rory went into the bedroom to change. Gloria peeked inside the bags.

"Peking duck is delicious plus there's some red pork stuff with fried rice, regular rice, and egg rolls. She saw two types of wontons. There were also soup containers. It looks like dinner will be a feast."

She turned and talked to the cat.

"Don't send Rory to a takeout restaurant on a hungry stomach. He buys twice as much."

Rory walked from the bedroom to the kitchen.

"I heard you talking about me. Please dish up the food in my normal large bowl. The food smelled good while I was at the restaurant. I picked up their packet of condiments. They have some new sauce the restaurant is trying. They told me the new sauce is hotter."

Gloria groaned and grabbed their bottle of soy sauce from the refrigerator. She wasn't into the wasabi or whatever hot pepper was in the new packets.

She fixed their bowls, and they ate dinner together in the den.

"There still is no word about Dillon's disappearance. I'm getting worried."

Rory took a drink of ice water.

"Man, this sauce is good."

Gloria resigned herself. There would be no more discussion about Dillon. Her husband didn't want to spoil his good mood. She would let her private thoughts roll.

She didn't tell him about Johnny's suspected necklace being in Clark's hands. Tomorrow she would call Dan to see if he could contact Zander's relative. Gloria wanted to know if the necklace was still part of Zander's property when he was found or in his apartment.

Next, she felt guilty for not communicating with her husband. Gloria put the leftovers in the refrigerator. Rory went into the den with the cat following close behind.

Before she went to bed, Dan sent her a text. The relative found no gold necklace in Zander's returned personal effects from Vienna or at his apartment.

She realized the feather may, indeed, be very real.

45 Car in a Field

The retirement notice was submitted by Gloria to her ballet company. She talked to the director about Tanya being a good fit for the second dancer position. She was told that Tanya moved to San Francisco Bay and joined the ballet theatre group in the city.

She thought Tanya's moving was odd because the dancer never contacted her. Gloria was sure they were friends. She asked the other dancers if they talked with Tanya before she left. None of them had done so.

"This is not like Tanya. I wonder why the hasty exit. The San Francisco company wanted her to start right away, and the money was good."

Gloria was busy with her new instructors and their classes at her dance studio.

One day Tanya's mother contacted her. The mother hadn't heard from her daughter for over three days. The mother contacted the San Francisco Bay ballet people, and Tanya never showed up for work. Then Tanya's mom contacted the new apartment people. Tanya paid her down payment and three month's rent in advance. The apartment people checked the rental space and found only empty rooms. Gloria's name and phone number were listed in Tanya's dancing notebook with five stars which is why the mother called."

Gloria met Tanya's mother at Tanya's old apartment. The manager there gave them Tanya's mail. There was a receipt from the moving company for transport to San Francisco to a storage facility. In rechecking the email, they found the invoices from the storage company. The mother called and paid the storage invoices and changed the payment to her address.

Gloria urged Tanya's mother to file a missing person's report. Neither Gloria nor Tanya's mother wanted to contact Clark. Tanya must have told him goodbye before she was going to travel to San Francisco. Tanya's car license plate was given to the police.

A week later, a farmer plowed his fields of corn. He found a vehicle in a lower field and contacted the police. The car belonged to Tanya Adams. An autopsy was performed, and it was determined she died from a drug overdose.

Gloria and her mother couldn't believe the report. Tanya didn't take drugs that either one of them knew. Gloria worked with Tanya who was always drinking green vegetable juice at lunch or crunching on carrots. No carbs or meat products were on her diet plan. The woman didn't own a bottle of aspirin in her medicine cabinet. Plus, they didn't understand why she would be 125 miles north of New York City. There was no reason for her to drive in that direction.

Rory, Gloria, and Dan plus a lot of other ballet people went to Tanya's funeral. They didn't see Clark there. A bouquet of red roses and yellow lilies stood to one side. Gloria took the card from the holder.

When Gloria and Rory reached home, she was naturally upset and depressed. He tried to comfort her in her grief.

"Why do we keep going to dancer funerals? This is unreal. Someone is responsible."

"I know. I met Tanya when I picked you up once, and she seemed fine to me. We can't understand because no one knows what did happen to her. Maybe her life was a royal mess."

Gloria looked out the glass window at the rain. The window washers cleaned them the day before. Now there would be streaks once the windows were dry. She watched the children playing in the park below. She turned to Rory.

"No, we talked. She loved to dance and wanted to make the second dancer position in New York City. Instead, she picked San Francisco. She was extremely involved in her career. Her career was everything. Dancing was the dream. Men were part-time play. That doesn't sound like someone contemplating suicide."

Rory looked exasperated.

"I didn't mean suicide. I imagine the possibility exists. Her death could be an accidental overdose. People forget how many pills they might have taken."

Gloria disagreed again with her husband.

"You are wrong. She knew what she was doing. Every step was calculated. Someone out there knows what happened. I think the person should be held accountable."

Rory knew that Gloria was referring to Clark.

"We'll let the police handle any conversations with Clark. Edwin told me about the box theory. I don't want you to go to Clark's home. Also, don't put yourself in the box by interfering. You could get hurt. If this wasn't an accident, I don't want you in someone's sight. Promise me!"

She looked at her husband. There was a possibility the killer knew her motives. She could be in danger no matter what Gloria did.

"What if the person comes after me?"

Again, she didn't mention Clark's name.

Rory's eyes turned to a dark smoldering fire.

"This person better not come after you. If Clark was involved in any way and tries something funny with my wife, he will see the end of a gun barrel. No, count that lots of gun barrels. I'll call Edwin's friends plus your father's."

She was silent and suddenly afraid. The killer could come after Rory.

"Make that two-gun barrels at minimum at all times," responded Gloria.

Rory knew his wife was trained. She went to a shooting range for a year and shot at the paper target to relieve some of her frustrations regarding Jordan.

"You just reminded me. I have bought you a weapon to wear when Edwin, me, or your family aren't protecting you. The gun is small and won't kill. It will maim if you shoot at the legs or eyes. Legs are easier. There are also the guns I showed you at the studio and the ones in our home. I'll ask Edwin to take you to the shooting range so you can try out this one and the style of guns I purchased."

Gloria looked at the small derringer and the crafted leather case with a belt.

"I'll need to wear my socks over the gun case."

Rory went into their bedroom and brought out a pair of her socks.

"Try the items on so we can see if any parts of the leather need adjustment."

Gloria did as she was told.

"I need one more hole in the strap and the end cut off by two inches."

Rory removed the gun, case, and belt. He put the belt in his briefcase.

"I'll take care of the correction tomorrow morning and let Edwin know you have the device."

The next day, Rory gave her back the redesigned belt. He wanted his wife to be prepared.

Rory tried to downplay his wife's theories about a killer in their midst. He was beginning to believe she was in danger more than before. Too many events were unfolding that jangled his nerves. Rory told Edwin to be on the alert.

"The recent events have made me look twice at people walking past Gloria on the streets. I'm on the alert. The first person that tries to hurt her is going down permanent-like."

Rory felt a little bit better.

A picture of Tanya's car in the cornfield was in the local newspaper surrounded by police cars. The police were hoping the picture would produce witnesses.

The ballet company decided to change the door lock codes for the dancers. They didn't like a newspaper photo of one of their dead dancer's cars.

Gloria contacted the flower shop. The flowers from Clark showed the paid date.

The flower shop clerk paused, "We have to order the yellow lilies ahead of time. They usually take two to three weeks. I'll ask the manager to find the exact date when we ordered the lilies."

Gloria thanked the woman. The date the flowers were ordered mattered. The flowers could show premeditation. Again, Gloria kept silent about the flower idea.

She awoke in a sweat one evening. There were people on the walls. Gloria shook her head and felt Rory's warm body sleeping beside her. The nightmare vanished. Going into their kitchen, she grabbed a glass of milk.

"Bad vibrations."

46 Studio Visitor

The last group of dance students left her studio. Rory was at a meeting in the city. Edwin called her because he was having car trouble. Edwin's wife was going to drop him off at the studio.

Gloria checked with the guard at their front entrance to let him know she was going to do one last dance routine and that Edwin would be arriving shortly.

She turned the lights off. Gloria was completely in the dark. Using the remote, she started the video. She spoke softly into her microphone when she was turned from the camera.

"Spotlight."

The light showed her illuminated body in the fifth position. Her movements were exaggerated and slow at first.

"Triple spotlight to progression."

Each movement went through the next spotlight on the floor.

"Almost full blur."

The shadows on her feet slowly faded as the floor filled with light. She moved faster through her dance routine. She was at the end part of the dance when a flash of rainbow light crossed on the floor. Gloria believed Edwin had arrived. She completed the dance.

The music stopped. Bowing to a fake audience. She rose and counted to five.

Gloria spoke to herself.

"We've got to get the door either tinted or frosted to eliminate the rainbow flash on the wood floor."

She would have to ask Rory to delete the flash again from the video. The sun on the door was brutal this time of day.

"We could put a cover over the entryway. Great idea."

She turned to see Clark standing fifteen feet away from her. Her heart was already racing from the exercise. Gloria's throat felt dry. Her body tensed.

The video and sound were continuing to run. She didn't look at the sound system but looked at the man.

He clapped loudly.

"Clark Reine? What brings you here to my dance studio?"

Clark looked around the room. He knew they were alone.

"Impressive studio. You have come a long way. Rich husband bought everything in here or was it the movie star dancer? He liked you as I recall. Tough luck for him. You wouldn't know where Dillon lives? I need to chat with him. You were a better dancer than Bella."

Gloria didn't know how to respond.

"I haven't talked to Dillon in years."

Clark continued speaking.

"Too bad. We should have danced together. Now things won't work. I quit dancing as Tanya told you. Oh, I stopped by the florist shop and talked with the manager. A person named Gloria made inquiries about my floral bouquet selection for a funeral. I only know one person named Gloria. I made a quick assumption. How clever!"

She needed to respond, "I was curious about where someone ordered the yellow lilies. The flower is quite pretty with ruffled edges."

"You are lying. Your curiosity was when they were ordered."

Gloria glanced at her watch. She wanted to explain.

"About the car, Tanya told me one day about the expensive sports car. When I ran into her at a department store recently, she was trying to do an exchange on a pricey necklace. I didn't have to ask. She said you gave her the necklace. The design is quite unusual. We are dancers and naturally talked. I was saddened by Bella's murder and now Tanya's death. You weren't at Tanya's funeral. I found that extremely odd because of your dating. The flowers were a strange choice."

Clark moved a few steps closer. Gloria picked up her water bottle and took a drink. Her logic provided him a reason for the curiosity. He wasn't buying her explanations.

"Tanya stole the necklace. I didn't realize she took the necklace from where I hid the gold chain. I accidentally saw her photograph and the text message that she sent you. You would naturally remember who owned a necklace just like that one. Zander's necklace was something that should have been left. You would naturally go to the police. Why didn't you?"

She looked at Clark, and there was a knife in his hand.

"The flowers were ordered before Tanya's death. I still wasn't sure until this very moment. Now I know you murdered your wife and drugged Tanya. You used to love Bella. I don't understand why you needed to kill her. Tanya was young and talented. There are always choices."

Clark's eyes squinted.

"The knife worked as did the drugs."

Gloria needed to stall to give Edwin time.

"Tanya was new, and you could have walked away. She didn't deserve to die for stealing a necklace that had already been stolen."

"I would have let Tanya go if she hadn't taken the necklace," explained Clark.

Gloria shook her head. "Oh, no. Her mistake was stupid and yours was more wrong. Zander was a little creep. You don't kill bugs his size. I don't understand except now you are here bothering me. Tanya and Bella's deaths are tragedies caused by you."

Clark turned the knife in his hand and watched the sun hit the sharp blade. Gloria knew that she was running out of time. She tried to keep him talking while she moved closer to the chair.

She put her foot on the chair to adjust her stocking. The snap on the gun strap released.

"Bella wanted a divorce. She was having an affair with a dancer. I'm a dancer. She didn't need another one. She wouldn't tell me the dancer's name.

Everybody thought she was a saint. She wasn't. As for Tanya, she was a mistake from the beginning."

Gloria realized what transpired. Bella and Tanya saw what she now witnessed. The man before her was devoid of feeling and love. The man was a major narcissist. Right or wrong was not in his vocabulary. She was talking to a robot. A human being didn't exist. The man was a monster of major proportions.

"Bella made me the laughingstock of the century. She wanted out of our marriage. Geri's murder helped me make my decision. The police would follow the serial killer's path if my wife died. Another dancer went from this earth."

"And Tanya?"

"Tanya's murder was easy. When she came to say goodbye, I refilled her favorite green drink. She was pleased I remembered the brand. Then I asked for the necklace back or the money. She couldn't return the money. Served her right for being a thief."

Gloria looked at the clock on the wall. Rory would be leaving his meeting. It would take him twenty minutes. She wondered where Edwin was in the city, and why the garage guard wasn't doing his rounds.

Clark noticed her glance at the timepiece.

"Your garage guard is unconscious in the trunk of my car. We'll dispose of him later. Now I need you to walk with me to my car. You can join the guard. If you want, I have some medication you can take. When they find your body, they will believe you were depressed. You took the meds to end your life. What a remarkably effortless way to die? Another depressed dancer went from this earth."

She couldn't believe the man.

"How could you copy Geri's murder with Bella? You are insane. I won't ever end my life with drugs. Everyone knows me. I will fight you."

Clark stared at her and watched her eyes as he raised the knife higher. He saw a flicker of fear and then a show of strength.

Gloria shouted angrily at him.

"You won't get away so quickly. You killed two of my friends. I want more answers. Talk to me!"

He shrugged.

Clark didn't care. He wanted to see her crawl. He could wait before he killed her.

"I need to know about Johnny Zander. You killed him for the money and a stupid necklace?"

Clark heinously laughed.

"The money was in a bag. He bragged about knowing the man's name in my wife's affair. Zander wouldn't give me Dillon's name at first. Only when the stupid man knew he was going to die did he reveal the name. Dillon's money was useful."

Gloria grabbed hold of the small gun on her leg and moved the safety button off. She was in major trouble with the stranger in the room. Clark was going to kill her. It was time to step out of the box.

"Dillon is still missing from Vienna. The boat you rented missed the mark, and he went to Africa. He liked strange places."

Clark's face grew red. He thought Dillon drowned.

"You don't know he's alive."

He watched her expression. Then he saw the blinking light.

"Well, well, what do we have here. There's a light on this fancy machine. Do you suppose the questions and answers between us are recorded? More cleverness! The video will be missing, I'm afraid."

He raised the knife to smash the light.

Gloria's voice screamed.

"Stop it, Clark, I have a gun!"

Clark turned and saw the small object in her hand. He laughed harder.

"You call a derringer a weapon. I'm blown away."

He laughed again more harshly.

Gloria moved toward the wall where there was a hidden drawer with a larger gun.

Clark was done with the conversation. His madness surfaced. She saw the personality change. A Bipolar disorder didn't even come close to the man's transformation. The man was evil incarnate. Her determination increased. She could stop him is what played in her head.

He leaped toward Gloria.

The dangerous man forgot something important.

She saw Clark dance many times before. She was waiting for the leap. She knew which foot he would use to land. She fired twice at his right leg, and he fell hard onto the wood flooring.

The man moaned. The knife weaponry went flying across the polished wood floor.

Clark was closer than she remembered. He quickly grabbed her leg and twisted. She moaned and dropped the derringer. Gloria was in immediate pain, and she fell. She kicked at him harder.

He grabbed her other leg.

Edwin arrived at the dance building a few moments before the derringer fired. He saw the guard was missing when he arrived. His wife already drove away.

Gloria's bodyguard withdrew his gun and texted Rory on his cell with the two words, an *intruder*. Then he heard the derringer fire. Edwin punched in the door code and entered the building. He flew up the stairs to the studio as fast as he could. Edwin threw the inner door open cracking the glass.

The noise made Clark stop pulling Gloria toward him. He loosened his grip when he turned toward the door.

She kicked free, crawled out of the killer's range of closeness, and raised her body. She jumped to the gun drawer. Her body fell softly against the newly stained and polished wood cabinet.

Clark went for the knife on the floor. The derringer slid under the wood display case. Edwin saw what was happening. Clark captured and lifted the knife in his hand.

"Drop the knife or I'll shoot you dead, mother sucker!"

Clark looked at Gloria's bodyguard.

"Mr. Sherman is here to save you. His presence is unexpected. Now we have a party of two people to kill."

Gloria punched the buttons, pulled the large gun out of the drawer, and touched the lever. Her gun was fully functional. She turned.

"Do what my bodyguard says Clark, or we will both blow you to bits. But then, you've already been to the Devil's Inn. Not to worry, we can send you right back. The parties there ought to be death-defying nightmares repeated overly much. I hope that I am right. Oh, and no more dancing for you."

The murderer saw the two guns pointed in his direction and heard the police sirens. He didn't have much time to escape.

Clark hated the female dancer, Gloria, in those last few moments. She was brave like Bella and Tanya. He killed them. Seeing that Gloria was closer to him, she would die first. Clark turned in her direction and leaped toward her with all his fury.

There was the bigger steel in Gloria's hands, and bravery exuded from her eyes. Clark didn't care if she fired the weapon. He was sure that as a man, he was more powerful. He was wrong. There was no hesitation.

Gloria and Edwin both fired their guns. The sound was loud. Clark fell at her feet. Gloria moved her foot away from his outstretched hand. The man on the floor didn't move. The bullet to the head worked. Edwin hit the heart.

Rory burst through the door and another piece of glass fell to the floor. With his gun drawn, he faced his wife and her bodyguard. Both guns turned toward him. Rory raised his hands.

Gloria and Edwin lowered their guns.

"Man, I thought you both were going to shoot me. What the heck happened here?"

He saw they were in control of the situation, and relief washed over him. The studio looked in disarray. Rory pocketed his gun.

Neither Edwin nor Gloria acknowledged his presence.

Gloria stood perfectly still. She was staring at the dead body. Edwin approached her.

"We jumped out of the box, Gloria. Together we brought the bad man down. Now, hand me your gun. You can walk away like in the old film story. We talked about the story with your father and Stan. Remember? You are safe in the dance studio. Rory is waiting."

Gloria's bravery vanished. She no longer felt in control. She shakily handed her gun to Edwin. Edwin put the large gun on the shelf and did the same with the derringer. He pocketed his gun for when the police would arrive.

Gloria awoke from her bad dream. Rory was waiting.

He stepped toward his wife. She ran into her husband's waiting arms.

"Oh, God, Gloria, you were right. I was beginning to believe your theories. I should have figured this one out sooner."

Relief flooded her brain.

"I know you were coming around to my way of thinking. I didn't want to be right. I hoped this day wouldn't happen. When he told me Geri's death inspired him to kill his wife, I became angry. Then he drugged Tanya. They were two beautiful women. They were dancers I worked with. They were like me. They dreamed."

"I know."

Rory tried to console her.

"After he admitted to killing Tanya with her green drink for taking Zander's necklace, I lost it. I know they were in this room giving me their strength to fight back."

Rory hugged his brave woman.

"You fought back, and I love my crazy wife. But let's not do this again. I can't lose the person I want to stay with for the rest of my life. You are my life."

Edwin kicked the knife out of Clark's dead hand, picked up the remote, and turned the video off. Rory knew the entire scene was videotaped.

The police rushed into the building. Edwin's other security personnel followed. Rory took out the video and handed it to the officer in charge of evidence.

Rory moved Gloria into the dance studio office to let the others clean up the mess. He was glad the weekend was here, and their studios would be closed. The police unlocked Clark's car trunk to let Randall's garage security guard go home. One of Edwin's company guards stayed to watch the garage for any intruders.

Rory and Edwin found a large board for the door and locked the building. They took Gloria home.

She didn't want to go to bed. Rory held her with the cat and a soft blanket. Finally, her eyes closed.

Gloria briefly stirred and spoke with a murmur, "I want the pickle packets."

Rory remembered Atlantic City.

"You can have mine, sweetheart."

He felt Gloria relax.

Rory held his wife closer. The cat licked Rory.

"You know we caught the bad guy. He was a thief and way more than we thought. Gloria took him out. She is a superhero today. We need to let her sleep."

Mara meowed, relaxed, and closed her eyes.

Rory did the same.

There was no need to worry about the evil person. Gloria's husband could watch the second copy of the video that was stored as a backup on the studio's hard drive. Tomorrow and the revealing video could wait. Now was more important.

Rory felt lucky and blessed. His heart and Gloria's heart matched from day one when they first met. He would do everything in his power to save her from unsavory crazies. He knew her family and friends felt the same way.

He told her, "I love you and always will."

Gloria snuggled closer to his warmth.

"Now I can stop chasing evil people. I couldn't rest and let the man get away."

Rory sighed.

"I hate when you play the heroine."

"No, you don't."

"Hush, go to sleep," said Rory.

She looked at her husband and the cat.

"You are here. I'm lucky, too."

Gloria finally let go and drifted to sleep.

Rory knew this last episode was too close. He was delighted his wife knew how and where to shoot. Edwin would receive a bonus from him.

47 Australian Text

There were more dance classes and instructors added to their studio. Gloria only needed to manage things from a distance. She spent most of her days at home.

Rory told her to take her time before doing any teaching. The trauma of killing a man was wearing off. She was feeling better. Gloria heard the knock, and she let her father and Stan into the apartment.

Stan put the two large grocery bags on the counter. Her father handed her the bag of rolls from the bakery. Stan left to get the last bag.

"We bought the nicer pan in case you want to cook again. The recipe book has some nice pictures. The potato peeler was in the most unusual of places in the store. Someone hid the thing behind the strainers. Then Stan found this cool device to grate lemons."

"Thanks, dad. I know the lemons will work with the chicken. I bought them yesterday from my neighbor. He has a few dwarf lemon types of trees on his balcony."

"Do you want me to help with peeling the carrots and potatoes? I'm rather good at doing the job."

Gloria debated.

"No, I need to learn how to cook proper meals for us."

Her father picked up the peeler.

"I can at least do half of the potatoes and half the carrots. Stan can do the other half. That way you can take your time learning."

Once completed, Stan and her father left.

Gloria was busy reading the cookbook and looking at the rest of the vegetables. She pushed the stuffed whole chicken in the oven for thirty minutes. After the buzzer rang, she grabbed the bowl. Next, she added the peeled potatoes and vegetables.

The meal should be done when Rory opened the door. Wrapping the bakery buns with butter in foil, she put them aside to wait for later. The buns only needed eight minutes.

A strange text came across on her cell phone. She heard Rory punch in the door code. He walked into the kitchen with a bouquet and champagne. He stopped and smelled dinner cooking.

"I could get used to the smell of homemade food. Is this a once-in-a-lifetime deal?"

He opened the oven door.

"I see a whole chicken, potatoes, and vegetables. Not to worry, I'll get the butter and sour cream. We'll make gravy next time. I'll help. My mom showed me how to make gravy."

Gloria held up the cookbook.

"One hundred and fifty pages of the real stuff is right here. There's even a gravy recipe. We could learn how to cook together. I have placed a bookmark in the thick porterhouse steak page."

He grabbed the cookbook and found the marker. He read the recipe.

"My turn next week. This looks fantastic. Where do I buy horseradish sauce?"

Gloria went to the refrigerator.

"Stan and my dad volunteered to do my shopping. They bought a jar. They also bought steak sauce and jarred garlic. I think they might like to be our dinner guests next week. They told me about the market on the corner which has good zucchini and tiny yellow squash."

"I'll make a note as a reminder to get the steaks from the meat market next Monday. The place has rafts of kale and goat cheese. Maybe there's a nice veggie dish in the book."

Gloria wasn't sure her dad would eat kale. The goat cheese was out for sure.

"We might try some other vegetable and good parmesan cheese. I'll put the items on my grocery list."

The buzzer went off. Rory helped her take the pan out of the oven and cut the chicken. The food was arranged on the countertop.

They sat down to their gourmet chicken meal. When they were finished, the dishes were placed in the dishwasher, and the leftovers were stored back in the refrigerator.

Rory brought them each a cup of tea. He told her the meal was delicious. Rory looked at his newspaper. Gloria opened her text and looked at the two pictures. She read the words; *the dancers were here.*

Gloria giggled and handed her phone to Rory. He scrolled down the pictures and handed her back the phone.

The two pictures showed a tanned man in a loincloth wearing colorful beads and long hair braided into dreadlocks. His face was painted, and he was holding a spear. Alongside the man were four darkly tanned children posing like dancers. The next image was two kangaroos behind a fencepost that read Sydney, Australia.

"Dillon Andrews is alive and well, I see."

"Yes, isn't that wonderful? He told me once he swam for exercise rather than use barbells."

Rory looked at his wife and kissed her soft lips.

"I suppose you want to take our next two-week vacation and go to Sydney for a visit?"

"I would like to visit Dillon and talk to him. Thank you. You will be okay with my being around Dillon after everything that has happened?"

"No, but I'll manage. No dancing with him. The man holds you too close."

"Kissing is fine?"

Rory grabbed her. He remembered the marble lips.

"Positively, not."

Gloria smiled.

"I'm glad you liked my lemon chicken dinner."

"I'm a huge fan. We can try the chicken next time with spicy sauce."

Gloria drank a sip of her tea and moved closer.

"No."

Rory's face fell.

"Maybe just a little bit."

"Does this mean I have to compromise regarding the kissing?"

Gloria thought about the question. She needed to live with Rory in peace.

"No, I would be afraid of what Dillon would send me next."

"Am I ever glad you are on my side," commented Rory while smiling.

Gloria knew she made the right decision.

"All jokers aside, when do you want to travel?"

Rory knew he would have to be specific on the date. He already checked his calendar when he was waiting for her bouquet.

"How about we go there for our anniversary?"

Gloria was pleased he remembered.

48 Sydney Visit

Their airplane landed at the Sydney Airport, and they met Dillon in baggage claim. Alongside him stood a pregnant woman.

"Hello Gloria and Rory, this is my fiancée, Miranda. We're getting married while you are here. We officially invite you to our very casual beach wedding this Saturday at the Rand Hotel at four o'clock in the afternoon. No need to rent a tux."

Gloria couldn't help herself and hugged Miranda. Next, she hugged Dillon.

Rory shook hands and slapped Dillon on the back.

"Congratulations. I'm glad to see this beautiful woman has decided to take a gamble."

Dillon didn't mind the dig. He was used to Rory's comments. They went to their hotel and ate dinner.

The next morning Rory and Gloria had fun playing tourist. Then they went to a kangaroo preserve and took pictures. They dressed for the wedding.

Gloria was glad she packed a casual long dress at the last minute. The dress was white with exotic flowers. The slits were high, and the gown showed thin straps at the top of the bodice.

Her husband whistled when he saw her. They sat in white folding chairs with a large group of people.

Gloria knew many of them were dancers. She could tell just by the way they walked and talked. They were pleased to meet an American dancer who knew

Dillon. She learned that Dillon belonged to the ballet company in Sydney. His soon-to-be wife was a doctor.

Dillon and Miranda met when Dillon had a bad fall and required a doctor who knew about foot bones.

Gloria and Rory watched the ceremony together. Rory squeezed her hand.

Miranda wore a blush long gown with pink flowers in her hair. Dillon was dressed in white slacks and a blush jacket and shirt. They walked together on palm fronds spread on the sand to meet the minister under a flowered arch. Their vows were simple and sweet. A violin quartet played soft music before and after the ceremony.

The reception was a large roast pig with trays and trays of vegetables and fruit. There was no cake in existence. The newly married couple chose small cups filled with fresh pineapple and coconut shavings.

There was dancing on the beach, much conversation, and partying under a large white tent. They were glad their dancer found someone.

Most of the wedding guests went home.

It was late but Dillon wanted to talk to his two friends. He told Rory and Gloria that it took him some time to get over Bella. He confessed that he genuinely loved her.

Dillon told them the moment he realized that Clark meant to kill him in Vienna, he changed. He realized love was a fragile thing.

There was a freighter that took him on as a worker. Otherwise, he wouldn't have been able to escape. The freighter crew was taking a new dinghy out for a spin when they found him sitting on the dock in the dark. He had a slight gash in his arm and was bleeding.

They took him back to the freighter where their medical technician on board sewed the gash. Then they helped him retrieve some clothes, wallet, and passport from his apartment.

Fortunately, he took out extra cash from his bank for a vacation before the accident.

He rode the freighter for a year before finally landing in Sydney. In Sydney, he found a job tutoring the children in a small village.

Dillon kept watching the American news and buying the New York City newspaper in the hopes that Clark would be caught for trying to run him down. He was shocked to learn that Clark was indeed the murderer of his wife and another woman.

Dillon felt guilty about leaving Vienna. If he told the police about the bad man, Tanya still might be alive.

Once he knew Clark was dead, he sent Gloria the text of pictures from his previous job in Sydney.

The couple said goodnight and promised to stay in touch.

49 Rory and Gloria's Decision

On the drive to their hotel in Sydney, Gloria put her head on Rory's shoulder. He was glad they were in a limousine that Dillon provided for them.

"I talked with Miranda. She seems nice. She is expecting a little boy. I'm sure Dillon is excited about the baby."

Rory hugged his wife. There would be no child for them unless they did adopt. He thought about their life together. Both were settled in their careers. He needed to approach adoption with an open mind. Rory struggled with the concept. He knew Gloria would be fine.

"We could contact the adoption agency when we return home. There's no reason to hold off from making this decision. Unless you are going to keep running into the bad people, we might have to hold off."

Gloria was happy Rory was thinking about a baby. She was hoping he would want a little girl. As if reading her mind, Rory took out a pink flower from one of the wedding tables.

"I like pink and little tutus."

Gloria's smile was wide when she looked at him.

"I guessed correctly?"

"Perfectly on the mark. I could teach her ballet." Rory laughed.

"I can see her ballet shoes. They are handmade out of very pricey silk."

Gloria squeezed his arm. She knew her father would be pleased.

"Do you have a name?" asked Rory.

Gloria had no clue.

"We'll have to work on the name."

"I like Gloria."

She thought about calling her daughter.

"No, the names would be confusing."

"How about Ria?" asked Rory.

"I'm liking the sound very much."

They arrived at their hotel. Both would be happy to return to America and begin their search for a girl child.

A half a year later, they would find their Ria who was six months old. An entire room in their condominium showed new baby furniture.

Gloria put her daughter on the large island. The cat jumped up and watched the baby while Rory seasoned the steaks.

"Look, Ria smiled at the cat."

Gloria frowned and the baby smiled again. She didn't tell Rory their child had been smiling for a week.

She picked up Mara and put the cat on the floor. They were eating in the kitchen as a family. The cat jumped on top of the refrigerator, crawled in the basket, and took a nap. The players knew the routine.

While they were eating, Stan and her father knocked on the door. Gloria grabbed two more plates and Rory got the extra steak out of the refrigerator with the salad.

Stan put four large potatoes and a packet of butter and sour cream on the counter. Her father opened the bakery box and took out a cherry pie. The whipped cream was put in the refrigerator.

Her father went over to talk to Ria. The baby smiled.

"She's been smiling at me for a week now. Ria knows who loves her best."

Rory looked at Gloria. She nodded.

Stan bumped her father out of the way.

"Don't pay any attention to Guy."

Rory flipped the steaks. Gloria knew their child was going to be spoiled.

"Do you think it's too early to teach her to dance?"

All three men responded, "Yes!"

Gloria would have to wait.

The doorbell rang and Rory accepted the package from the delivery boy. He saw the package was from Edwin addressed to Ria.

Gloria opened the package. Inside was a ballet costume with a skirt in azure blue. The little belt buckle was a tiny light that you might put on a dog to wear outside at night. Gloria turned the tiny switch and held up the costume.

The men went, "Aww!"

Gloria shook her head, laid the costume over her Ria, and touched her baby's feet. Their little girl kicked happily.

"It was a moment and a person had to be there."

Rory took a picture and posted the image to their social media website.

In the next few weeks, they received more outfits of varying sizes up to four years old. There would be no need to buy tights or costumes for Ria. Gloria was busy the next two weeks writing personal thank you notes.

Rory would watch their daughter while Gloria taught a class. They installed a window in the office door so the students could wave to Ria. She didn't seem at all afraid of an audience.

Dillon saw the photo and sent Rory and Gloria a picture of his son, Alan. He wanted to know if their children would ever dance together in the future.

Rory picked up his sweet little girl.

"Not until she is forty years old, and then I'll have to think about it."

Gloria sent Rory's response.

Dillon replied.

"Is this guy still carrying a grudge against me about the stunt in your hotel room?"

They sent Dillon a picture. The picture was their cat, Mara, holding a sign that read, "Men's underwear sale. Look for a huge box from your friends at the old dance troupe."

"Oh, no," texted Dillon, "I've got to intercept the package!"

Rory and Gloria knew they finally got even. Their life settled down until they decided to buy a little dog.

"The dog fits in Gloria's gym bag," was posted on their website.

Dog tutus arrived in the mail. The dog sat next to the baby as an extra guard.

Rory was busy letting Stan and Edwin's daughters pet the dog and take him out for bathroom breaks.

They put extra soundproofing in the walls between their condominium and the neighbor's condominium.

The cat could leap around the place without ever touching their floor. The two creatures tolerated each other.

At night, Rory had to move the cat and the dog out of their bedroom to be with Gloria.

He asked her, "Were we a little crazy to get married?"

She looked at her tired husband.

"I'll stay home tomorrow. You can have a quiet day."

"Thank you. I have a better idea. Let's drop them off at your father's place, so we can be alone."

Gloria slapped his outstretched hand.

"Good idea. On second thought, Stan can watch the dog. Mara will think we gave the dog away."

50 Grand Stafford Ballet Company

Gloria tied Rory's necktie. She stepped back, and her husband looked charming in his new tuxedo. He pulled his wife close and held her.

She wore a gold dress that sparkled and flowed around her slim body and legs. She wore an emerald necklace he bought her with diamond earrings.

They were going to the Stafford Theatre for their Grand Stafford Ballet Company's seasonal performance.

"I'm so glad our twenty-one-year-old daughter Ria made the ballet company. Now we can sit back, relax, and enjoy ourselves. We get to sit together in the dark."

Rory looked askance at his wife.

"I will enjoy sitting with you in broad daylight or the dark."

He drove his sports car to the parking lot where a valet would park their car. They walked to the theatre building. Rory stopped to read the marquee of dancers.

"There is her name, Ria Randall. I'm so proud of our daughter. Let me take a picture. You stand in front of the sign."

Gloria did as she was told. A couple joined them.

"Rory, why don't you step next to Gloria, and we'll take another photo."

Rory put his arm around his wife and looked at the camera. The man holding the camera paused.

"You're not smiling Rory. Give me a cheesy look."

Gloria looked at her husband. He turned to look at his wife and smiled. The person took several pictures and handed the camera back.

"Very nice camera. Hello, Gloria, you look amazing in gold and emeralds. But then again, you looked good in a green and blue leotard outfit long ago. I still remember."

Gloria replied, "Hello my dear friends. Do you want us to take a picture of the two of you with the dancer's sign?"

The woman answered, "No, we took pictures yesterday. We must hurry to our seats. We don't want to miss the opening dance. Our son will be the lead dancer."

The couple hurried off. Gloria watched her husband. He sighed.

"I guess our meeting them outside wasn't so bad. I was cordial, don't you think?"

Gloria knew he was trying.

"I explained your reactions to our daughter when she told me who she was dating."

"You mentioned the dynamite that might be handy for me to use and the lie about your soft kisses?"

Gloria squeezed her husband's arm.

"We should go inside and see our daughter dance with Alan Andrews."

They settled in their seats. Rory spoke.

"I would hate to have Dillon as a relative. Should I talk with our daughter and warn her away from

Dillon and Miranda's son? There are lots of other good dancers she should meet. I'm hiring a new photographer next week. He said he was single."

Gloria jabbed him with her elbow.

"Ouch, your answer is a mean and flat no."

She gave him a look. The show announcer came out.

"You need to let her make up her mind. She is legally old enough and a very independent woman. She can date and marry without our approval."

"There are benefits to waiting until she is forty."

"Rory."

He knew that tone from his wife. It was time to be quiet. Rory waited for the curtain to open. They watched the ballet performance until the formal intermission break. He leaned over and whispered to his wife.

"Ria dances like you. Super pretty and let's not mention that she floats in the air when she jumps."

"Yes, she was an excellent and very astute student. Extremely competitive as well. Alan dances like his father, don't you think?"

Rory stood up.

"Let's join them downstairs for refreshments."

Gloria was glad to stretch her legs. They would see their daughter at the party at Gloria's 1,2,3,4. A huge party was planned. The Andrews were invited along with many other dancers.

"I'm glad you finally agreed to play nice. The party tonight should be fun."

Rory gave his wife a quick kiss and gently took her hand. He and Gloria were happy with their lives. It was time to let their child soar, have some fun, and allow her to find her way. He hated letting his daughter go.

Miranda and Dillon were waiting for them inside the lobby with Guy, Edwin plus his wife, and Stan and his wife. Dan was there with a new male friend. Edwin and Stan's daughters were also in the ballet company as secondary side dancers. The group would see them at the catered party. Edwin Sherman's security company would monitor the grounds and parking.

Miranda pinned flowers on Rory's jacket. Dillon fumbled with the flower on Gloria's dress.

"Oh, for heaven's sake, man. Give me those flowers."

Rory shoved Dillon aside and pinned his wife's flowers to her dress in three seconds. The flowers were a red rose and a yellow lily with green ferns in remembrance of Geri, Bella, and Tanya.

"There you go sweetheart," said Rory.

The waiter brought their champagne-filled glasses, and they did a toast to the three female dancers no longer with them.

The group did small talk pleasantries about the weather and the flight from Australia.

Gloria's eyes widened. Behind Dillon stood an actor in a tuxedo with a clown wig and makeup. Dillon turned and almost dropped his glass. He looked at Rory who was smiling evilly.

"Rory, I will get even," mentioned Dillon sarcastically.

Miranda and Gloria put their glasses down and walked to the restroom.

"We knew your husband was going to do this move. Thank you for the warning. We hear Rory has a new sports car which will be parked behind your dad's place."

Gloria smiled.

"Thank you for the warning. Don't you wish the two boys would grow up?"

"I doubt we will see those moves happening in our lifetime. However, we can be good friends. I enjoyed the other day."

Gloria said, "I did, too."

The women joined the men and returned to their seats for the final performance.

After the performance, Rory and Gloria drove to his studio. Gloria was surprised when they parked in the guarded garage. Rory escorted her to a large van close by. The van contained the Randall's Dance and Photography logo and sign.

She looked confused. Rory opened her van door. Edwin was already in the back.

"Get in. There's no way that I'm going to let Dillon near my new sports car. I ordered the van on purpose for our party. I thought whatever Dillon was planning could happen on the company van. If he ruins anything, I can do a tax write-off. I've never trusted the man. He's up to something. He wasn't shocked by the clown."

"How did you ever guess?"

"Do old dogs ever change their colors? The correct answer is no. They get stronger."

"Are we talking about a little paranoia setting in during old age?"

"I'm not that old. He's the prankster."

"Really?" said Gloria.

"I've also hired one of our photographers for the event. I thought we could use the pictures for a press release celebrating our beautiful daughter and her wonderful parents." Rory looked at his wife.

"I will await the story. I'm sure the evening is not over. I'm glad my father invited a few of his police friends."

"You mean that I had better behave?"

"Just this once. This party is important for our daughter."

"I don't know if I can cancel the gold bikini mannequins."

Gloria gave her husband the look that said you are dead meat.

"I was just kidding."

Rory reached over and grabbed her hand.

Gloria believed the evening was just getting started. She knew a secret that she hadn't told Rory yet.

Her father encouraged her to inform Rory about the engagement. After the change in a vehicle and their discussion, she decided to wait.

The white silk wedding dress was hanging in Rory's studio for their daughter's wedding to Alan. Ria's nametag was on the stuffed hangar with the sales ticket. The white gown was expensive and was inside a beautiful white satin and a cotton-lined cloth bag with the designer's name splashed across the outside.

She saw the mischievous look on her husband's face. There was no reason to change his fun for this evening's party.

Ria and Alan hadn't yet told Dillon. Alan suggested they keep the engagement secret a little longer.

Ria, Gloria, and Miranda helped select the wedding dress and shoes. The three women went shopping because they knew the best stores in the city.

The wedding would take place in six months. Gloria worked with a travel agent to arrange a two-week vacation with Rory after the wedding.

There was next Monday to deal with first. She would need to calm him down when he opened his studio's closet door.

The women hung white paper tissue bells, white streamers, and a garter belt in the doorway and left the closet door open. The white garter belt contained a gold piece of jewelry. Two metal ballet dancers were attached. They thought Rory could figure out the message.

Fortunately, the elderly Randall's wouldn't see too much of Dillon and Miranda until the wedding. The Australian couple planned to leave New York City and staying in Sydney.

Rory and Dillon would have six months to get used to the engagement.

The party was winding down. The crowds of people were dispersing. Rory came to the table where Gloria was sitting.

"Another nice party at your dad's place. His friends are great. I am so glad he finally fixed the parking lot problem in the back. The tar is much better. I got tired of my sports car coming to the condominium with dirt from the bistro."

"I noticed the new sign out front."

"Did you now?"

"My father said you fought city hall to go larger and paid for the new sign."

"I reminded them my wife brought revenue to their city and was a homegrown child star. They were lucky you still lived here."

"My dad showed me your incredibly convincing letter."

"I wanted the name Gloria to be bigger and then we needed a revamp of the neon dancer with her legs in a more beautiful position."

"Thank you," said Gloria.

Rory was a happy man.

"I need to confess. The travel agent left a message at your studio about the tickets to Australia and our daughter's upcoming wedding. I looked around your and my studio. I also saw the closet."

Gloria looked guilty.

Rory bent and kissed his wife.

"I'll get used to the change. I promise. You shouldn't keep me in the dark. Can we go home now?"

"Yes, dear. I like you in the dark."

"Not fair," chuckled Rory.

Gloria held out her hand. "We can go home."

"Your prince waits for his dancer."

He escorted her to the front door. A white limousine awaited.

"The horses and carriage were already rented. However, I've secured a spot for our anniversary party."

Gloria took her husband's arm. He whispered in her ear.

"I'm here always."

Gloria knew he would be.

Author's List of Books

Blue Dancer and the Dark

Purple Queen and Lost Charm

Knight Detective Series:
Book 1 - Gray Area for a Woman
Book 2 – Pink Sky in the Morning

Orange Carousel and Orchid Murders

Black Horse and Female Lawyer

Green Emeralds and Heist Club

White Boom and the Seagulls

Gold and the Spotted Jaguar

Raiment Red and a Raven –
A Southwest Mystery

A Wright Series:
Book 1 – Diamonds Blondes and Poison
Book 2 – Dead On Coordinates
Book 3 – Wild Golden Obsession
Book 4 – No Easy Target
Book 5 – Powerhouse Race
Book 6 – Cross Paths